Kidnapped By Consent

Mickey from Manchester Series, Volume 27

Mike Scantlebury

Published by Mickey from Manchester, 2024.

This is a work of fiction. Similarities to real people, places, or events are entirely coincidental.

KIDNAPPED BY CONSENT

First edition. August 28, 2024.

Copyright © 2024 Mike Scantlebury.

ISBN: 979-8224803613

Written by Mike Scantlebury.

Chapter ONE: Down the stairs

"Tell me again, Mickey," the Police Inspector said.

Again? Mickey had made a statement already. Then he repeated all he knew.

How could he add any more? There was only so much to tell.

"Sorry to trouble you," the policeman said. "But this is serious."

Yes, he was right, Mickey was thinking. Of course it was 'serious'. Eighteen people had disappeared.

But what did Mickey know?

Only that he had been dragged from his bed that day, by an insistent phone.

"Billy needs your help," a voice said.

Mickey's blood ran cold. He had been dreading such a call.

He knew the voice. It was Trevoir, a man he had served with in the Army, many years ago. They had been pals, more than friends. When you've lived together, under canvas, relying on each other, watching each other's back, you had a bond, he thought.

Trev lived in the North East now, Mickey knew. It was hundreds of miles away, amd they hadn't met up for ages.

But Billy - He was a younger man, younger than themselves. He had been like the 'baby' of the Unit, they all kept saying, and everyone made a special effort to look after him. It hadn't worked. He had been blown up by an Improvised Explosive Device, and been rushed back to Britain for treatment to his legs. He spent months in a Cambridge hospital.

"He's living near you now," Trev told him that morning, and it was a surprise to Mickey.

He hadn't heard from young Bill Budman for a long time, but then, he hadn't bothered asking.

I'm a coward, Mickey was thinking to himself. Somehow I imagined that if I didn't frame a question, then I wouldn't get any bad news answers. Mickey was ashamed of himself. They had been close - each one of the men. Why was Mickey hiding now?

Trev gave Mickey an address. It was in Central Manchester.

Mickey gulped. Behind Picadilly railway station? Melia had a flat in that area! Mickey knew it well.

Of course, that was just one more reason to feel bad, for Mickey, trying to get fully awake.

He hadn't seen Melia for monhs, and hadn't bothered about it. She was busy, he knew. He was busy. Good Grief, they had lived together for a whlle! Everyone assumed the affair was still going on, and Mickey let them think it.

What have I been doing, Mickey wondered? He had no good answer.

Days passed, weeks went by. Who knew where the time went?

But Trev was telling him things now, and Mickey was making an effort to fight off the brain fog.

Of course Billy would want to come back up to the North West. He had been born there. If he was able to make that move, then maybe the doctors had finished with him. Maybe he was well. He had a flat? Maybe he could cope.

"He phoned me," Trev told Mickey, "but I've got a family thing today. Can you help?"

Mickey did what Trev expected him to do. He said 'Yes' without thinking.

Of course he would. They were all old pals.

"It sounds simple," Trev said. "Bill said he wanted to get to a Public Meeting. It sounds important."

Mickey was still trying to concentrate. It was Saturday. Anything could happen on a Saturday. It was a favourite day for activities in Manchester - marches, protests, Meetings and gatherings. What kind of campaign was Billy involved with?

"It's a Planning issue," Trev told him. "I haven't got any details."

Mickey nodded at that.

He had once been heavily involved with the Corsh Corporation, the biggest property developers in the region. He knew that 'Planning' might seem like a small thing, but it could involve rebuilding a whole district, clearing property away or building it.

The area behind Piccadilly station was one part of Manchester that was steadily being replaced. Was that it?

"The Meeting's in Salford," Trev told him. "Down by the river."

Mickey lived in Salford now, but not south, not by the river. He was in North Salford, a traditional area, with old houses. Mickey liked it. It had shops within easy reach, parks and countryside nearby. He felt comfortable there.

"You've got time," Trevoir told him.

It was true.

Mickey was able to have a lazy shower, pick out some clothes that might be acceptable to be out in public, as opposed to lying around the house, and even have breakfast. Toast, cheese, tea, he soon felt better and more like himself.

He would take the car, he decided.

Parking in central Manchester was a challenge, he knew that. There were multi-storey car parks, but they were expensive. Still, he had an idea. Melia had given him a set of keys, once, when they were together. A key for the front door to the building, a key to her flat, but, most important of all, a fob for the underground car park to her building.

Mickey chuckled. Worth it's weight in gold, he was thinking.

He drove down Bury New Road and around the Ring Road. It was slow. People going into town for shopping? It was a weekend. Still, he had allowed for delays - and building works. That was the main problem. So many high-rise developments in the centre of the city, roads were blocked, with scaffolding encroaching on pavements and pathways. He was barely moving in the middle of town. The cars were nose to tail. Still, when he came off London Road and let himself into Melia's car park, he was feeling pretty pleased with himself.

He had the address.

Billy lived on a nearby street, around a few corners.

It was a flat in a low-rise block, maybe four stories. Bill was on the third floor.

Mickey took a deep breath. I wonder how long he's been here, and I never knew, he was thinking.

Maybe I'm not such a good friend, after all.

There was a set of bells and buttons on the street door. Mickey pressed Number Seventeen.

A little screen lit up. A video picture.

It was Billy Budman.

"Come on up," he said, without a 'Hello' or greeting.

He buzzed the front door so Mickey could get into the lobby. There was a lift, and stairs. Mickey took the stairs.

At least I'll get a little exercise this morning, he was thinking.

He knocked on the door that said '17' and there was a rustling behind the door. It opened.

Billy was in a wheelchair.

"Come on in," he said briskly, and moved back. "I'll just get my phone."

He was washed, dressed. He looked ready for the world.

Mickey took a few steps forward. The apartment was neat and tidy, everything in place and clean.

He couldn't help staring.

Billy Budman turned and saw the look. "It wasn't the bomb," he said briefly. "I survived that. They got me walking again. What would you think - just in time for the neurological disease that is destorying my muscle functions."

Mickey couldn't conceal his surprise - surprise and grief.

"Bill, I'm so sorry - " he began, weakly.

The handsome young man brushed the words aside. He didn't have time for pity.

He said: "We can talk about it later, Mickey, when we've got a spare minute. Right now, you can help me. I need to get to that meeting. It's a huge development in East Salford. They're planning to demolish shops for apartment high-rise blocks."

Mickey nodded. If there were shops established on site, then it wasn't 'brown field', derelict. The proposal was to destroy existing facilities and simpy swap 'Retail' for 'Housing'. He seen a few of those in his days working for Corsh.

"Let me get past," Billy snapped, not at all the diffident youth he once had been.

"You want a push?" Mickey offered, but Bill just scoffed.

He wheeled himself out into the corridor and approached the lift.

"Just pull the door behind you," he told Mickey, and the apartment was secured. "I'm pressing the buttons."

But that wasn't so straightforward. The buttons didn't respond.

Mickey moved up and stood alongside his pal.

"The lift's broken?" he asked, starting to feel concerned.

"It was installed by the Anglo-American Elevator Company. What do you think? It's not reliable."

Billy wasn't surprised then, but he was angry.

Many a time he would plan to go out, then find the lift wasn't working. So he would be forced to turn around and abort his journey. This time he wasn't about to be put off. This was an important Meeting, vital. He decided he needed to be there.

"That's why you're here," the youngster told Mickey. "That's why I called for help. You'll have to guide me down the stairs."

He stood up, shakily, and started pulling himself along the rail by the wall, towards the stairs.

"Stop!" Mickey said, coming to life at last. "Stop, darn it. If I'm here for a reason - "

He leapt forward and swept up his pal in his arms. He didn't weight more than a sack of potatoes.

Taking a deep breath, Mickey backed into the door to the staircase. It looked a long way down.

"Don't drop me!" Billy yelled, a little worried, maybe.

Mickey was big, he was strong. He was often mistaken for an unfeeling brute, but that was only on his off days. Other times, he could be quite feeling. Like now. I have the muscles, he was thinking, and now I'm going to use them.

He didn't stumble, all the way down the stairs, but by the time he reached the ground floor, he was sweating freely.

He propped Bill against the wall by the door to the street and took several breaths.

"I'll need my chair," the kid reminded him.

"Of course you will. Of course you will," Mickey said, and started back up the stairs again.

Then all he had to do was retrieve Bill's wheelchair, bring it back down, install the youngster in it and push the kid up the road, around the corner and down into Melia's garage. The chair folded. It went in the back of the car.

"Where's this?" Billy asked. "You live here?"

"A friend," Mickey corrected him. There would have to be a lot of explaining later.

Mickey drove them around the Ring Road, then turned up into Regent Road, a main route out of town.

"Sangford's Supermarket is over on the right," Billy explained. "There's a car park in front of it, then, on the north side of the cars, there's a line of shops - clothes, a pet shop, a pound 'Bargain', a chemist's and a coffee shop."

Mickey nodded. He knew the area. He'd often parked his car there for a coffee and a small shopping expedition.

Bill said: "The supermarket is staying, and the parking in front of it. But everything north of the access road will be swept away. New, enormously tall blocks of apartments will be put in. At least five. We've been promised a grass walkway, maybe some trees."

"Why's this important to you?" Mickey asked, thinking: He's living in the centre of the city, massive Manchester now.

The kid said: "During the Second World War this whole area was Council Housing. My grandad was born here."

Mickey was following directions to the Meeting. They turned left, then left again.

Billy said, musing: "The Council flats had huge cellars. I can just imagine my gran's family sheltering there from the bombs."

Mickey nodded. It was pretty emotional, but logical? No. Salford Council had built apartment blocks there in the nineteen thirties, then swept them away in the 'fifties? Shops had replaced them sure, but not pretty shops. It was all these 'sheds' - just big, square, open-plan things with the air-condtitioning pipes showing in the ceiling?

But here they were, dragging themselves out of bed to meet up with fellow protestors and create a storm, hoping to block the proposals? Maybe there were better ideas in mind - a park, a leisure centre? Perhaps a swimming pool.

Or just say 'No', was that it? The Meeting didn't want anything new. They just wanted things to stay exactly the same.

Well, that was their right. They could have their point of view, promote their opinions.

That was no reason for eighteen of them to be kidnapped.

Chapter TWO: Into the trees

"I haven't heard the whole story," Captain Gibson told Mickey.

Mickey sighed.

He had gone over and over the events of that Saturday afternoon, and it still made little sense to him - especially the way it turned out. But what interest could the Captain possibly have in the mystery? Gibson was the boss of TEEF, the foremost anti-terrorism unit in British Security. It had formidable resources and personnel - in fact, Mickey had once been a valued member of the team.

But now Mickey was retired - or, at least, he thought he had left. Strange how new events kept dragging him back.

Of course, he DID have to come back if the Captain asked him to. That wasn't just doing the old man a favour - it was some sort of clause in the Official Secrets Act that made Mickey liable for recall. Also, he partly enjoyed it, seeing his old chums.

Captain Gibson, it was true, had never been a 'chum'. He was far too straight-laced for that. Thin, wirey, with a brutal pencil moustache, he was every inch the 'Old School', and though government Ministers might come and go, Gibson persisted.

Despite the change of venue.

When Mickey was with the Unit they had the use of an old, dilapidated-seeming warehouse in the old part of Salford. But one particularly vindictive foe had burned that location down. Terry, the computer expert on the team, was given the chance to research something better. He came up with a brand-new office block, or at least, part of it. The top few floors of the base for a major television company on Salford Quays.

When that place grew too hot - and the subject of a TV documentary - Terry came up with an even more off-the-wall idea.

The Unit members would hide 'in plain sight'.

Each operative, or small team, would rent a room in the old Chelsea Mill, near Chapel Street in Salford. The original building was more than two hundred years old, but had been divided into offices and workshops, of various sizes. The TEEF staff would 'blend in', Terry assured them. They would appear like any other small business owners, with small offices and a computer on the desk.

Terry though, he inisted, needed a double suite, for all his equipment.

It seemed to be working quite well. So, when Mickey arrived at the Mill for his 'business meeting' with the man in the smart suit, jet black hair and ramrod straight deportment. Mickey was happy to go along with the illusion that Gibson was someone in Insurance, and he was a client, there for a sales pitch.

They met in the courtyard of the main Mill building. There was a small vegan cafe there, and they could sit outside in the sun. It was a warm summer's day, unusual for this part of North West England.

Mickey started talking, and didn't stop for the first round of coffee. Then they ordered another.

"We got to the church," Mickey had said, "where the meeting was to be held. I got the wheelchair out of the back of my car and Billy practically leaped into it - he was so keen not to miss anything. I let him roll himself in - it said 'Disabled Access' on the door - and got talking to a man standing around. He told me he was a driver, a professional paid driver. I looked around."

"This car?" Mickey asked him. "This big, black one?"

"Nah," the man said, grinning. "That's the Mayor's limo. You know, the 'Ceremonial Mayor', who gets to wear the gold chair and the ermine cloak for a year. Maybe they tour around all the schools and playgroups."

"Where's the elected Mayor?" Mickey asked. His pal, Sol Senate. He'd had dealings with him in the past.

"He's a 'No Show,'" Mickey was told. "Maybe he's busy, cooking the books and selling off all the Council assets."

Mickey feigned shock. They might say such things round here, he was thinking, but he trusted his pal Sol.

The man went on: "The MP's here. I think her husband brought her."

The 'driver' pointed out an unostentacious saloon backed up against the wall.

Mickey had met her too, the Member of Parliament for this eastern part of Salford.

Rachel Scot-Mott. She had principles too. Mickey had a lot of time for her.

"There must have been Councillors too," Gibson blurted, breaking into Mickey's flow.

Sure there was, but Mickey wanted to drag it out. He wanted to tell things as he found out about them.

For one thing, it helped to explain his surprise. There were some big guns at this meeting, important people. It wasn't just a bunch of 'NIMBY' residents. They had some high-level support. That was impressive.

One more thing.

Before he went in, Mickey had asked one more question.

"What are you driving?" he asked the 'driver'.

The man chuckled. "This is my rig," the man said, turning to indicate the long vehicle behind him.

It was a minibus, and it had a logo along the side. Something like, 'Radcliffe Academy'. Something like that.

Mickey nodded. Impressed.

"I bet you could get 14/15 inside there," he said. It was a long one.

"Eighteen," the man assured Mickey.

At that moment, Mickey didn't know whether the little bus had been employed to bring people TO the meeting, or was going to be used to ferry them away. But, strangely, that was one of the first things he found out.

As he came to the door of the meeting, the heavy oak door into the church, people came boiling out.

Complaining.

"You haven't answered any of the questions," an angry local woman was shouting at a smartly-dressed young man in a suit.

"And that's why you need to see for yourselves," the younger one said smoothly.

Mickey didn't get it. He thought the whole meeting was all about an idea, an architect's dream. A set of drawings.

Billy came wheeling up to Mickey's elbow, to head him off, to reassure him he didn't need to go into the church.

Bill said: "They're putting on a trip for us. A coach tour. They say they have a 'similar' scheme nearby, and want to show us."

A man in waders was standing by the door, unconvinced. "It's a Con Trick," he kept saying. "Don't believe it."

The minibus driver didn't seem surprised.

He shouted: "Room for seventeen, plus me."

"I'm going in my own car," the beligerent woman said.

"Where is it?" Mickey asked no one in particular.

"South of Stockport," Billy said eagerly. "Come on, Mickey. Help me into the coach."

Bill said that he wanted to travel with his new 'friends' and insisted Mickey help him up the steps, fold the chair and put it in beside him. The driver didn't complain - which was unusual - and was happy to assist.

Mickey said to his pal: "I'll follow in my car, Bill. If you get fed up, just wave and I'll take you back to your flat."

Billy waved that aside. He was having far too much fun.

The young man, the smartly dressed young thing in the suit, said: "Me and Geraldo will lead the way in our car."

It was a sports car, fast, expensive, red. The kind of car you don't have to open the door to, you can just jump right in over the door.

Mickey scanned the crowd.

He noted that the Ceremonial Mayor was making her escuses, saying she had another ceremony to attend.

The MP was whisked away by her husband, presumably on another mission too.

The other elected Councillors didn't make such a convincing jog of being busy. They slunk away and disappeared.

All in all, it seemed like it was all local residents clambering into the painted minibus. Walking along, Mickey saw that there were two empty seats at the back, but the rest of the vehicle seemed filled.

The strange convoy - extrvagant sports car, school's minibus, two black cars, and Mickey's - made their way out of the stone gates and onto the road. They turned right, then left, and headed for the road to Stockport.

So far, Mickey explained, it didn't look suspicious at all.

But the A6 South is a long, busy main road, going through suburbs and shopping streets before it reaches open country.

The vehicles soon got split up by other vehicles and lost sight of each other.

Mickey realised, with mounting horror, that he really had no idea where they were headed, not at all.

Until his phone rang.

It was Bill. He was sitting close behind the minibus driver and the man was shouting instructions over his shoulder.

Mickey calmed down, and followed directions, as relayed.

On the other side of Stockport, a big town, Mickey veered left at a junction and found himself heading uphill into a forest.

Now this was silly, Mickey was thinking. The proposed development adjacent to Sangford's supermarket was in an urban area, not the middle of the countryside. A pretty little village of cottages would look nothing like the plans Billy Budman hated.

Mickey was noticing the road was getting less wide. The trees were closing in.

He tried phoning Bill for further information, but the minibus wasn't replying.

Mickey was thinking: Did they say 'straight on'? Were there meant to be twists and turns?

He was rapidly losing faith in his own remembering, when a strange thing happened.

Around the corner, in front of him, a bright red sports car slewed around the corner, TOWARDS him.

The car slowed and one of the occupants leaned out and yelled: "Keep going! Look for the crossroads!"

It was the two young men from the meeting. What were they - architects? Planners? Landscape gardeners?

They seemed well trained, well qualified and confident. Mickey could almost have faith in them.

Except for one thing: he had lost the minibus, (the little coach), and the other following cars, the black ones. And when the road started running downhill and came out of the trees, there was no sign of a crossroads. He drove on, nonetheless, and before long came back out onto the main road. In ten minutes he was in Buxton. That's when he knew he had gone wrong.

"I lost them," Mickey admitted to Gibson.

"They became lost," the Captain agreed. "And haven't been seen since."

Which is the whole nightmare, Mickey was thinking, not sure what it had to do with him, or what he could do.

"I want you to work on this, Mickey," Mr Gibson told him. "It could have Security implications."

Could it? Mickey wondered. Maybe abroad, in sandy countries. People were kidnapped all the time, but Britain?

The Captain added: "You'll need someone else to work with you. This is a big one. You'll need a team."

As if by magic, or some sort of curious tip-off, a young man in uniform came walking through the gate to the street and approached the table. Gibson greeted him warmly and invited him to sit down. The boss gave a wave of his hand, imperiously, and a waitress appeared. Orders were invited and coffee was offered. Mickey demurred. He thought he had achieved his quota for the day.

Gibson said: "This is Inspector D. de Angelis. He has joined our Unit, temporarily. You have met, I know."

Mickey was nodding, but his heart wasn't in it.

This is the man who had previously kept him awake and stretching while searching his memory for nuggets he'd forgotten.

"Will our colleague be sacificing his old employment when he starts work with us?" Mickey asked politely.

"Not at all," Captain Gibson said smoothly. "That's why we need him so badly. A man INSIDE the police force."

Mickey wasn't thinking of the advantages of having a spy on the inside. His mind was drifting in a totally different direction.

Wow, he was thinking. TWO salaries.

Chapter THREE: Missing something

Gibson was back in his office when Terry the computer guy came to see him.

"Mysteries aren't really my area," Terry told his boss.

He was clutching a tablet computer and seemed eager to share.

"You just missed Mickey," he was told.

"Well, yes," Terry agreed, "this is his kind of thing."

Gibson chuckled. "He's just about up against it with his own mystery," he told Terry.

"Well, then, I don't want to overwhelm him," Terry smiled, "but this is a brain bender."

Gibson odered the young computer expert to pull up a seat on the same side of the desk, so that they could both see the screen. That was unusual behaviour for the Manager of TEEF - he usually liked to have the solid wooden slab between him and visitors, but he could see that Terry was looking completely stumped, and *that* was unusual.

What was more likely in the Unit is that Terry could solve every known computer problem under the sun, and run rings around his colleagues. With his wild red hair and thick glasses, he was everybody's idea of a 'nerd', and he was happy to play up to it.

The day he said he was baffled, therefore, was likely to be a very bad day for the Unit.

Terry said: "I've got a couple of short videos."

He teed the first one up, and let it run, but for less than a minute.

It showed Jerry Garage, the leader of the MEGA Party in Britain, an outfit that had done well for themselves in the recent election. Jerry, or Jerczy as he had been known until recently, was riding high on a wave of euphoria and congratulations.

In fact the first thing the man had done, once the votes were counted, was fly off to the USA to visit his inspiration.

That big man, a candidate for the forthcoming Presidential Election in the States, was happy to be photoed with Jerry.

"My big buddy," the American was calling him, "from our biggest buddy in the world, good ol' United Kingdom."

Accordingly, the American called Jerry Garage, 'Jerry Gah-raj', in the American way. It sounded neat. Nice.

Mr Gibson had his own opinion about the garrulous US Presidential candidate, but he was happy that Anglo-American relations were so strong.

"I don't see a problem," Gibson said, seeing the British representative so well received.

"We don't think it's him," Terry said calmly.

There was a short silence while the Captain processed the problems of having a fake US candidate might bring.

"Mr Garage. Jerry Garage," Terry confirmed, to avoid confusion. "The body is only approximate - and the voice is good, very good. But the fact is that the real Mr G. is not in the USA right now. Nowhere near."

"So where is he?" the Captain asked, playing the cat and mouse game.

Terry clicked some buttons on the side bar of the tablet screen, and another short video popped up and started rolling.

This showed a rally, in a medium-sized hall, with cheering MEGA followers, in their distinctive green caps.

The man on the platform was a real rabble-rouser, and his stirring speech was ringing to the rafters.

"We don't think that's him, either," Terry said, killing the sound and letting his boss see the difference in movements.

The Captain said, "That's obvious. Jerry's been in hospital. He was blown up. Maybe he hasn't recovered properly."

"He never recovered from being dead," Terry said lamely.

At last, he was forced to confess. The thing that they had been keeping from the Captain, since before the British General Election - just to save his blood pressure. All the team knew that their boss wouldn't be able to cope with the Election in Britain - PLUS the last minute loss of one of the chief protagonists. So when Mickey reported that Jerry Garage was no more, they closed ranks.

"This is outlandish," the Captain said, for once, lost for words.

He didn't know? He hadn't been told?

Mickey's mission - given to him by a nervous Captain - was to infiltrate the MEGA organisation, get close to Mr Garage and somehow prevent him from starting a revolution in a volatile Britain.

Mickey had done all of that, and the culmination was that he was in a car, scooting up the M6 motorway northwards, following Mr Garage in a van with two bomb-makers, the younger and older Ian Bann.

Luckily, Mickey wasn't that close behind, so avoided getting caught in the blast when the van exploded while going under a railway bridge. The explosion was planned - by Jerry - but he hadn't calculated he would be in the van when it went up. The plan had been to push the bomb out the back. Ian Bann Junior had other ideas. He hated his Dad, and was happy to take him with him to Hell.

Jerry Garage, along for the ride, was just collateral damage.

When Mickey got back to Regional Headquarters in Salford, the team decided they would have to spin Gibson a line that 'Jerry had been dropped off a little earlier' and was only slightly hurt. He 'was in hospital, recovering'. When 'Jerry Garage' re-appeared in public, some weeks later, no one was more surprised than Mickey, and Terry, but the men had to keep quiet, since their boss was happy to believe that recuperation had taken place. and Mr Garage was back in action.

Of course, Terry could see it wasn't the real person, even then, but was forced to keep his worries to himself.

Now, since the election had come and gone, he felt more safe in revealing the ongoing duplicity.

Gibson needed to know about it because if anyone was going to do anything about it, it would be the Captain.

But he was dead, definitely gone, Mr Garage.

At least, Terry thought so at first.

Firstly, because Mickey had seen the bomb go off, and it destroyed the van, right down to its axles.

No human being could have survived that.

Jerry Garage was no more. So what happened? No surprise that MEGA would want to continue their crusade.

So they find a replacement. Obvious.

But then, even MEGA weren't that clever. They couldn't put their Dear Leader in two places at once.

"Check the dates on the films," Terry suggested to his boss.

Even Gibson could see that. It was the same date.

On two continents. The fake Mr Garage was being backed up by another fake Garage. Two of them.

At least, Terry was thinking, but didn't say. How many more were there?

There could be dozens.

Not to be outdone, one of Terry's staff was about to make affairs even more complicated.

There was a knock on the door, but it was peremptory. A young man came crashing in anyway.

"You need to see this, Boss," he said.

He was talking to Terry.

The new guy was, in many ways, a duplicate of his superior. He had the same thick glasses, and wild hair, but slightly more auburn. Maybe that was why Terry hired him - because he resembled his own good self - but it made it awkward for the rest of the team. Some of them, maybe the old ones, found it hard to tell the two kids apart. Maybe that's why they insisted on naming the newcomer Terry Two, to keep it simple. (Or maybe they simply meant Terry Too.)

This Terry, the new arrival, had a laptop computer in his hands and it was open.

Seeing Terry and Mr Gibson on the far side of the desk, he came round the side away from Terry One, brushed papers aside, and set up the screen so that they all could see it. There were people along a desk, and a crowd.

It was a Press Conference.

"The man in the middle," Terry Two explained, "is saying that he's an architect. He says he's escaped."

Gibson took a deep breath in. He was hoping the air would help his brain to function.

"Explain that," he snapped.

Number Two said: "The minibus disappeared on Saturday afternoon, as Mickey has told you. Mickey made it back from the trip to the countryside, as did the two black cars, with local residents inside. But the red sports car didn't. Our information is that the red vehicle contained an architect and a landscape gardener. The man hosting this press conference is asserting that he was kidnapped, along with the people in the minibus. Sixteen plus those two. That makes eighteen. Eighteen people missing."

"He's Found," the Captain said drily.

"The man said they're all being held in an old barn at a farm off the road to Buxton. He says it's a kidnap situation, and the criminals are demanding a ransom of five million pounds. He said he managed to get out a side door, when they weren't looking."

"Is that likely?" Terry One said, trying to picture the situation.

"The five million? Not really. No one else is saying that."

"Who would?" Gibson demanded.

"The kidnappers," Two explained. "There's been no demand for cash. No communication at all."

"No," One said. "Is it likely he could have slid out of a barn door and got safely back to the city?"

"Look at him," Two said. "He's been telling his story, answering questions. He says he's come straight from the train station. Look at him. That's the smartest suit I've ever seen on an architect, (so he must be doing well). But no mud, no damp. He's hasn't trekked across fields or crawled under a hedge. And no one kept count - like noticed there was only seventeen now?"

Gibson has a question. "What are the Police saying?"

"Good question. If you look at that 'panel', there isn't a copper amongst them. Everyone on the stage is a journalist, a reporter or an Agent. The Police weren't invited? One thing I know: at the Police Press Conference last night, the Deputy Chief Constable said that they had visited every farm along the Buxton Road. So where is this barn, full of minibus and passengers?"

Terry One shifted uneasily in his seat.

If that was the story, it could be checked. He could do it himself. He could get a bird's eye view of the area on his main computer and identify every building big enough to qualify as a 'barn'. Then he could zoom in and look for clues.

But there was a more practical point.

If some thugs were holding eighteen people prisoner, they couldn't keep them cooped up in a ban. They would need to feed the captives, find them room to lie down and sleep. Let alone go to the toilet. Don't mention toilets!

The Captain, meanwhile, had his own thoughts.

He was thinking about the Police. Darn it, we have a policeman on the case - the man I've allocated to work with Mickey.

Unfortunately, he didn't want to mention that to the two computer guys. He didn't know why.

"Right," he said, making decisions. "I want you to make a copy of this Press Conference, and as much supporting information as you can glean from the News media, and send it all over to Mickey. Tell him that it's his responsibility to involve the police. He'll know what I mean.

After that, I want you to divide your time. Terry, your team needs to keep on with monitoring MEGA, as we discussed, but you can delegate your junior to supporting Mickey's investigation. Make the split as you see fit."

The computer guys started heading for the door. Gibson was feeling relieved he was about to be left alone again.

Outside in the corridor, Two said to One: "I'd be happy to keep on this 'kidnap' thing for Mickey, Boss."

"Oh, and why's that?"

"This 'architect' fella. I've got a feeling he's a scammer, trying - somehow - to get his hands on a share of five million pounds. And, you know, I'd be more than happy to bring him down."

"Sure. Go for it."

"I guess," Terry Two said thoughtfully, "I don't like fakers. And, for some reason, I've never liked architects."

Chapter FOUR: More information

"I don't know your name!" the Detective Inspector told Mickey.

"I don't know yours," Mickey retorted. "Captain Gibson said you were 'D. de Angelis', but he didn't say what 'D' stood for."

"Dee."

It took a full minute for Mickey to process that information. 'Dee' could be a person's name as well as a letter?

The policeman said: "And you're called 'Mickey'? Just 'Mickey'? It must be Mickey Something?"

That made Mickey laugh outright.

"That's good!" he said. "Yes, I like that. I'll be 'Mickey Something'. That's a good name."

"Can I make you gentleman a drink? Tea, coffee?"

The speaker was a round, intense man who had introduced himself as the Church Warden.

The two investigators had returned to the church where the meeting had been held on that Saturday afternoon.

They were hoping to find some new clues as to where eighteen people could have disappeared to.

"Tea for me," Mickey said cheerily, and followed the man to the small kitchen counter in the corner of the room.

It was nice here, Mickey was thinking. The room had once been the rear of the church, but it had been split off with a light and airy barrier of glass panels and wooden surrounds. That was a good idea. There was still an old, impressive stone church at the front of the building, which was at least a hundred years old. The stone was red, probably local to the Salford area. Atmospheric.

"Something can have tea," the Inspector said, "but I prefer coffee, thanks."

While they waited for the kettle to boil, it was clear that the Warden was happy to talk.

In fact it was difficult to stop him.

"I don't think they planned an abduction," he told the visitors.

"How do you know that?" the police person snapped.

"Men talk," he was told. "They go to the toilet, they stand around, and they talk. It just so happens I was in the facilities when the two men from the development company came in. The meeting had been going on for at least an hour and it wasn't working well for them. People were asking too many questions and it was making them uncomfortable. One said; 'Let's take them for a ride. Put them in the vehicles, drive them around for a bit. They'll get bored, go home, and we're off the hook.'"

"But the 'tour,'" Mickey protested, "it was meant to be to another of their developments, south of Stockport."

"They have no developments in that area," the Church Warden said. "I looked up their company on the internet, before the meeting. They have schemes developing in East Manchester, near the stadium, but nothing south."

"Why didn't you say this to the police when they were here?" the Inspector said, irritably.

"You're the first policeman I've met," the man said.

Mr de Angelis shook his head.

"No, the uniformed coppers," he said. "The ones who were here on Saturday, after the vehicles vanished."

The Church Warden smiled.

"The cars all drove off and I locked up the church. Nobody came down to ask questions, not then and not since."

He methodically put stuff in cups and added boiling water. He handed out the drinks and took several deep breaths.

The Inspector lifted his cup and took steps back from the tea bar.

"Listen, Something," he hissed at Mickey, "there's something wrong here. The police should have been here and taken statements. This is a kidnapping we're talking about. Eighteen people. The biggest thing to happen in Manchester for years."

"You want my opinion?" the Church Warden said loudly, not coming out from behind his bar.

"Of course we do," Mickey said, realising there wasn't really enough at the moment to go round.

"That man on telly," the church guy said, his voice conspiratorial. "He said he was an architect. Maybe he is. But he isn't the architect who was here on Saturday. They have similar suits, but the one we had on Saturday had a beakish nose. Looked like a bird."

The policeman's eyebrows shot up in surprise, then he recovered. He hated conspiracies.

"Maybe they all look the same," he said, trying to placate the witness.

"I was here," the church warden reminded the policeman. "I saw the two men in suits. I made them tea, just like you."

"Then who do you think is sitting in Press Conferences, pretending to be from the company?" the cop asked.

"Well, then, I wouldn't know that," the Warden agreed. "I wasn't there. I haven't seen him up close. I have no opinion on the question. But I was here, and spent time watching the company guys squirm. They were sitting at the table, by the door."

Mickey said: "They were being asked probing questions about the development? They didn't know the answers?"

"Oh, they knew the answers all right," the church man laughed. "They just didn't want to tell anybody."

Mickey drank his tea. If this witness was corrrect -

"You weren't in the hall," the church warden told Mickey.

That's right. I was outside in the car park, Mickey agreed. I didn't get round to seeing the conversation.

But a picture came into Mickey's mind. Sitting in his car, on a country road. Leaning out the window and being shouted out by a young, smartly dressed fellow in a sharp suit. What did his face look like, Mickey kept thinking. Like a bird?

"We're floundering here," he told the policeman. "We are trying to explain the disappearence of a whole busload of assorted civilians, and we're not even sure who it was that led them off on a wild goose chase to Cheshire."

"Derbyshire," the Inspecter corrected him. If Buxton was involved, it was Derbyshire.

"Anything else I can help you with?" the Warden said cheerfully.

He seemed to be a man who was happy to relay facts and share opinions.

"What do you have in mind?" the policeman asked suspiciously.

"Well, I have the leaflets," he was told. "The two company men were sitting in the middle of the 'Top Table', answering questions - sort of - and waving their leaflets around. I saved the ones they handled. I thought you might be able to get fingerprints off them. You know, they could be useful, I was thinking."

"Fingerprints?" the Inspector exploded. "What the - "

"You don't know who that pair were," the church said reasonably. "Who knows - they could have been con men, scammers."

"What could they possibly gain - "

"Hold on, Dee," Mickey said, grabbing the cop's elbow. "This is the first real fact we've managed to uncover. Yes, mate, fingerprints are a thing. You're right, maybe the two suave men in suits weren't who they were pretending to be."

Five minutes later, the two investigators were out on the street.

The Church Warden had thoughtfully found them a plastic bag to put the 'evidence' in. The leaflets.

"H said the school was close," Mickey agreed.

They were moving on. They'd done the church and now they were trying another angle.

The minibus.

Mickey had suggested the vehicle had 'Radcliffe Academy' painted on the side (or something similar), but that school, the Church Warden told them, was along this street here, and out on the main road. 'You can't miss it,' he said.

The Inspector wasn't sure what they would do there. Maybe find out who was driving that day?

But the driver, Mickey pointed out, was one of the people that had been kidnapped. It's not as though he would be there!

Unfortunately, the visit proved to be disappointing.

It started well. The school was there, and there was a similar minibus in their car park, off the road and slightly lower down.

Two minibuses.

They walked alongside the fence towards the Main Entrance, which was behind pillars. A classical look for a new building.

"Four slots," the Inspector muttered.

The school car park was marked out in neat, white painted lines. Even and small for each car, and these were mostly full.

But there were four bays big enough for minibuses, and two of them were there.

"Four minibuses?" Mickey said, uncertain.

"It's a big school," the Inspector noted. Big, newly built. Lots of glass and chrome. Expensive to build? Easy to maintain.

It was a secondary school, for 11 to 18 year olds, the only one in the area.

The entrance was a glass door, but it was locked. There was a buzzer.

When Mickey spoke politely into the intercom, the door was opened and the pair of sleuths went in.

The Inspector wanted to go first, but Mickey held him back. I'm the charming one, he was thinking.

There were two ladies behind the desk, and sure enough, they were happy to greet Mickey.

Still, Mr Dee wanted in. He elbowed his way forward and showed his I.D., his Warrant Card.

The ladies bristled.

"You've probably heard about the kidnapping," Mickey said, smiling. "We just want to know about the minibus used."

They looked helpful, but confused.

"The minibus," Mickey said. Your minibus. It was 'kidnapped' along with sixteen passengers."

"You'd better talk to Ged, he's our driver," the younger one suggested.

"Here he is now," the other pointed out.

A grizzled man, thin and aggressive, came bustling up to the Reception Desk.

"Just out for a Field Trip with Year 8," he announced to the women.

"I am a Detective Inspector and I have questions," the policeman said, stepping in and blocking his path.

The driver looked the cop up and down, and paused, as if considering hitting him.

Maybe that was his usual response to police, Mickey was thinking.

Mickey said: "We're just checking. One of your vehicles was involved in the incident on Saturday afternoon.

The man seemed puzzled.

"You weren't driving," Mickey said, trying to be helpful. "It was the other guy."

The driver bristled. "It's just me and the teachers," he said, a little too forcefully.

The Inspector said: "Mr Something was there. He saw one of your vans, and someone else driving."

"A teacher?" the driver said. He turned to the girls on the desk. "Any of our staff got kidnapped?" he joked.

"He was black," Mickey said.

The man paused, but seemed happy to confirm facts.

"I'm not black," he said, sarcastically. "I know it wasn't me."

"I know it wasn't you," Mickey agreed.

"Look," the Inspector snapped, getting irritable. "All we're saying is one of your buses is missing - "

"No it's not."

"Theres's two outside," the cop protested.

"One of which," the driver said, "I will shortly be taking out. The other one has already been commandeered by Doug, the Games Teacher. He's taken the Swim Team to the Baths, as he usually does, this time of day."

"That leaves one - " the policeman said, labouring the point.

"Which is in the garage, being repaired," Ged the driver told the investigators. "It's waiting for a part."

"That makes four," one of the women said, anxious to help.

"All accounted for," the other said.

Mickey turned away.

"This can't be right," he whispered at the Police Inspector. "One should be in a barn somewhere, maybe on a farm."

The Inspector turned back to the desk.

"This is Radcliffe Academy?" he said, looking for confirmation. "You own four minibuses. No more?"

"No more," Ged agreed. "And now, gentlemen, much as I have enjoyed this conversation, I really must love you and leave you. Year 8 are desparate to go and see some flowers, and there aren't enough around here to spark their interest."

Mickey had a thought. "Where would that be, then?" he asked. "Where are you going?"

"The Bishop's Wood, up on Bury New Road. It leads down to the river."

Ged the driver tried to smile, spun on his heel, and departed.

The Inspector looked at Mickey.

"You appear stunned, Something," he told his colleague.

Mickey was. He had been surprised by the answer.

"I live just across the main road from there," he informed the Inspector. "I have a house. By the playing fields."

Chapter FIVE: More developments

At that precise moment, someone was knocking on Mickey's door.

A head poked out from an upstairs window next door. It was a tousled-haired woman.

"Will you please pipe down!" she yelled. "I'm trying to sleep."

"I've got a delivery," the man downstairs said. "One for you too. Important information."

There was a pause while the woman pulled her head in and disappeared. A few minutes later, she came out of her house,, pulling an angry dressing gown around her ample body. Her hair was piled high on her head, but her pretty face lacked make-up.

"I work nights," she informed the middle-aged, rounded man. She was angry to be disturbed.

The man was disturbed. He found the woman attractive. The fact she was half-dressed was a bonus.

"Don't I know you?" he asked obliquely, awash with hormones.

"They all say that, darling," she reassured him. "I'm a dancer. Once seen, never forgotten."

"Where do you perform?"

"Regularly? At the 'Korean Lotus'. It's a Club in the city."

"You work there?" he gasped, thrilled. "What's your name?"

"Lotus."

They were an odd couple to be standing outside Mickey's door, on a lazy, sunny afternoon. But the man had a job to do.

He had a bag slung across one shoulder, and it was full of glossy leaflets. He had a clipboard in his hands.

"What number are you?" he asked, trying to be professioal. He was told, and made a note of it.

He said: "Can I give you one for this house?"

She looked him up and down. He looked like a customer, she was thinking. Older, losing his hair, spreading out a bit at the waist. She was used to staring down at such men from her podium. They liked her. She was fun, blousy, seemingly easy to please.

She was taking them for a ride.

The lady took a leaflet for herself, opened it and gazed at the colourful pictures. As she turned it over in her hands, the collar of her gown fell slightly apart, and over her shoulder.

He'll like that, she was thinking giving him a show.

She would talk to him, she decided. She would give him her attention. Usually, it was something men paid for.

"What's this all about?" she asked, fixing him with her gaze. "Explain it to me."

The delivery man, feeling his pulse racing, was pleased to be of help.

"The pictures are an imagination of what's going to happen to this empty space here," he said.

He waved an arm to indicate the grassy area in front of the houses.

"The playing fields?"

She had chosen her house because it had what the Estate Agent called an 'open aspect'. There was nothing but grass for a hundred yards, out to the road, and beyond that were the woods, leading down the hill to the River Irwell.

To the man, it was nothing but a gap, an opportunity to be filled.

The woman looked at the drawings, in colour, of happy men and women strolling in the sunshine, under trees.

Around them, on all sides, were the yellow stones of new brick buildings, jumbled in all directions.

"These are houses?" she asked.

"Absolutely," he agreed. "The City needs five and six bedroomed houses."

"Who for?"

"Large families?" he suggested, weakly.

She considered. No, all in all, from her point of view, this was bad news.

Also, for Mickey.

Sure, she would accept a leaflet for him. She would let him have it the next time she saw him.

She liked Mickey.

The man saw that the lady wasn't pleased. He was terrified he was losing her, and tried to cling on.

"It will raise house prices around here," he said, hoping that was something she would want to hear.

"It's quiet in this street," she answered. "I sleep in the day. It's because I work at night. You're telling me there's going to be builders moving in, across the road here, tearing up the grass, digging holes and laying bricks. When shall I sleep?"

The picture that now filled his head - of this charming female, turning restlessly in bed - was almost too much for him.

"It's temporary," he suggested. "A two year scheme, at most."

"That's what they're telling you?"

"They're telling me, to tell you."

"Who are these people?" she asked idly, turning over the leaflet in her hands.

"They're called 'Henshykan'."

She saw the name on the back of the glossy page, at the bottom, in small print.

"I think they're Korean," he said, not really knowing who he worked for. "You should have no problem with that, considering where you work." She stared at him. "The Korean Lotus," he stumbled. "I thought maybe you would know the language."

"Ee kyo mon lalang pur lama sa neh doo do."

He gasped. "What does that mean?"

"You really do not want to know."

"No worries," he said. "They're very good at English. The residents will be kept informed, at every stage."

"If I can hear you," she said, smiling, "over the noise of the building works."

She was smiling at him. He liked that.

He knew their interaction had to end, but did it? He was grasping at straws.

"Maybe I'll see you at the Club. We can talk more. I'll explain it to you," he suggested.

She grinned at him, a little slyly.

"That would be nice," she said. "Buy me a drink and I'll sit with you."

He nearly burst apart with anticipated pleasure.

"One thing," she said, raising a finger, "bring lots of small denomination notes. I hate it when men throw coins at me."

He had no idea whether she was joking or not.

The problem is, he was thinking, I have to move on. There's more houses to visit, more streets.

Soon, she was thinking gratefully, he will go, and I will be left alone.

I shall return to my bed. Alone.

* * * * *

Four hours later, she was in her lounge, idly staring out of the window, when she saw Mickey walking up the street.

She rushed out to greet him.

"Hi, Den," he said warmly, genuinely pleased to see her.

His face fell when he saw the glossy thing in her hand.

"For me?" he gasped. "You'd better come in. I need a drink."

He liked his neighbour. She was charming, fun. They had spent many happy hours, talking.

Denise liked Mickey. He wasn't like the usual men she met. He didn't ask her for anything.

Mickey led the way into the kitchen at the back of the house. He put the kettle on.

She put the leaflet on the table.

Mickey pulled something similar out of his pocket, and laid it beside the first.

"What else they planning?" she gasped.

"I picked this one up at Melia's. I dropped in to her flat. She's away."

Denise knew Melia. She often came to vist Mickey. Sometimes she stayed for days, weeks.

They were both strong women.

"I've got a key. Of course," he said. "She likes me to pop in and check on her place when she's not there."

"So, you picked up the Mail?"

"There were letters, bills. Flyers all sorts. And this. A Notice of Intention."

"Well, someone has got 'Intentions' for us too, right here on our street."

Mickey said: "There's a name at the bottom of the page. 'Henshykan'. Sounds Asian."

She explained that the man delivering the things said they were Korean. Maybe.

"That can't be right," Mickey mused. "I was at a meeting on Saturday, and nobody said anything about foreign investment, in Manchester and Salford. It was all about local businesses, home-made millionaires."

"Yes, but look - I mean - Oh, that can't be right - "

She held the two bits of paper up, side by side.

"This drawing here, this 'imagined' future for our site - " she started.

"They're the same!" he agreed.

Same happy people, strolling beneath trees, under a blue sky, with the sun shining.

"In Salford?" she gasped.

"In Manchester?" he added, looking at his own brochure.

She looked intently at the one Mickey had brought with him.

"There's a map here," she said. "A tiny diagram. Well, that's odd. I know Melia lives on a corner, in a low apartment building. But they've outlined the whole block. Is that the plan? To demolish perfectly good buildings, just to build higher?"

Mickey demurred.

"Well, that's what they've got planned for the shopping precinct I heard about on Saturday. It's hardly 'brownfield' sites, either of them, any of them. They're taking existing buildings, flattening them, then substituting skyscrapers."

"This block," she said, again referring to the plan for Melia's building, "it includes the other street too."

Mickey looked. He hadn't been paying that much attention.

But then it struck him.

"It's Billy's building too!" he gasped. "My friend Billy. He lives in a similar apartment to Melia, but around the other side, another street entirely. I hadn't realised. The proposal is to take down the whole lot, including his property!"

"He's protesting?"

"He was there on Saturday," Mickey agreed, but that was about a completely different development. Billy hadn't said anything about the place that he lived in. He said it was all about the Sangford's site, not anything in central Manchester!

Mickey made mugs of tea, and the two neighbours sat thoughtfully in his kitchen.

Eventually, she said: "I told the man, the one doing deliveries, that it's not just the proposal for here - the pretty pictures, sure, but completely destroying our view - but the building time. He said it would take 'two years'. That's twenty four months of diggers, and scaffolding. Cinder blocks, and bricks. Builders shouting and swearing at each other - "

"It's not going to be pretty," Micky agreed.

"If we're going to move, Mickey," she told him, "we need to do it now, before they start."

Or fight it, Mickey was thinking. Just like Billy was doing.

But the thought occured to him. I could spend a year opposing the development, and then lose. But by that time the whole plan would be public, and there would be no chance of selling his house. Nobody would want to buy it, once it was clear it was being completely boxed in. The 'open aspect' would be gone for ever, and there would be nothing but brick walls to look at.

Yellow bricks.

"Wait," he said to her, "you could afford that, Den? A new house?"

She laughed, "I've got savings," she said. "Men give me money."

It made her thoughtful, but at last, she asked: "You talked to Melia about this?"

Mickey had to admit he hadn't. She was away, and he didn't know where.

"You secret agents!" she laughed at him. "Passing, like ships in the night. Never meeting up. Still, then there's your other pal, Billy. You discussed this with him? The two of them have pretty plum addresses there, right in the heart of the city."

"I haven't," Mickey admitted. "He's one of 'The Eighteen', kidnapped on Saturday afternoon."

"What? 'Kidnap'? Who?"

Mickey stared at her. "You must have read about it," he told her. "A whole busload of people - "

He filled in a few more details, but she still looked totally blank.

"Well, maybe you missed the News," he said, smiling. "But it's been all over."

"No, it hasn't."

Mickey had been so absorbed in the drama, he thought everyone would be bound up too.

She said: "Mickey, I follow all the News bulletins, offline and online. I make a point of it. You think I would miss a kidnapping, if it had been featured? A kidnapping in Salford, you say? So, who did that? you want me to find out. I know people, Mickey. Gangsters. People talk."

Mickey shook his head.

"Maybe it's a delicate situation," he suggested. "A difficult negotiation. Maybe there's a News Blackout."

"Yes," she agreed. "Maybe that's it. Or, on the other hand, they're hiding it. It's being suppressed."

Mickey didn't know what to say.

Why would anyone do that?

"Maybe it's a Conspiracy," she suggested.

Chapter SIX: Progress down under

Later that day, as it was getting dark, Mickey reported to Captain Gibson, in his office.

"Thanks for coming, Mickey," the boss told him. "I know your priority right now is the kidnapping farrago, but we've got this unsolved mystery of Jerry Garage, and it could affect the state of the new government. It could involve National Security."

"I've got a secure line to Australia," Terry announced, from behind the desk.

They filed round - the Captain and Mickey either side of the computer tech.

Mickey really didn't know what was going on. Who was on the other side of the world? How could they help?

"Mickey," Gibson muttered, "you think Mr Garage is dead, only because you were in a car, following a van up the motorway that blew to smithereens, killing everyone on board. You think you know that included Ian Bann, the younger bombmaker, and his Dad, the older Ian Bann, but Terry has got some News to share, and it's disturbing."

"The van was a total wreck," Terry admitted, "and there were no bodies recovered. But there was plenty of flesh. I don't want to be gruesome, but the lab has been testing the remains for months now. All the parts belong to the Bann family."

That's impossible! Mickey was thinking.

He didn't want to contradict anyone, but he knew what he had seen.

"Okay, Okay. Australia calling. Anyone hear me?"

Mickey looked up in alarm. It was ex-Deputy Director Caulfield, a man who had abandoned TEEF after that incident and moved back to his native Australia to resume a career in the local police force.

Mickey was amazed how Caulfield's Aussie accent had come back. So soon!

"Thank you for joining us, Richard," Gibson said to him, overly polite, considering what he really thought of his previous Deputy.

"No problem, cobbers," the man said, laying on the Australianisms. "I usually get up at six, and this is about right for me."

"You've gone back to uniform?" Mickey observed.

Caulfield chuckled. "I was in uniform in Hong Kong when I was there," he reminded everyone, "and in Oz here, before I started with you gallahs."

"That was a long time ago, Mr C.," Terry said, not bothering with formality, now the man had left the Unit.

"You might say," Caulfield went on, in his self-obsessed way, "that TEEF in the UK was the only time I was ever in mufti."

Sharp 'mufti', Terry was thinking. Caulfield was renowned for his sharp Italian suits and hand-cut loafers.

"I was just reminding Mickey," Gibson said, sterring the conversation, "that he wasn't alone in the car that followed the Banns. You were in there too, Richard. I hope your memory is clear."

"Clear as a lighthouse bell," Caulfield say cheerfully. "We were never more than fifty yards behind, for most of the way."

"What? 'Most'? What do you mean?" Mickey demanded, as if he was being attacked.

Caulfield said: "Well, there was the time we went off at the wrong junction."

Mickey started thinking.

In his head, he had been driving hard, focussed, concentrating. He had a picture in his head of the van in front of him, never too far away. The mission had been to see that the van arrived safely under the railway bridge and the bomb detonated. Everybody in the vehicle was meant to jump out alive, but, as far as Mickey was concerned, nobody did. Nobody.

Caulfield recalled: "We were nearly at the right place, but the van pulled off at the off-ramp. It went up the slope to a roundabout, paused, as if unsure of the way, then crossed straight over, and went back down onto the motorway, heading north. So, we had to wait at the roundabout for a moment or two - there was heavy traffic - and we lost sight of the van. I've been thinking about it. There would have been time for Jerry Garage to open the door and leap out, as the van went down the slip road."

Leap out, or get pushed out? Mickey was thinking,

But No, he still wasn't convinced. Maybe there was a moment - but what - seconds?

And why? Why would the Banns have wanted to ditch Jerry? Did they have a suicide pact and wanted to lose the witness?

Suicide? Even that was uncertain. Most people said, afterwards, that it was Junior who had set off the bomb, destroying himself and his Dad at the same time. Just before the journey he had found out unpleasant truths about the Old Man.

Maybe he wanted to kill him. Maybe it was a 'Murder-Suicide'.

Gibson interrupted Mickey's musings. The whole 'Why Bann' was no concern of his.

"We have a problem here, Richard," his ex-boss told him. 'Garage' people are making appearances all over. We need to know if that is required because the original is deceased. Or is it a temporary measure, while the damaged leader recovers from his injuries?"

Caulfield was enjoying his chance to be helpful. He loved being the centre of attention. He wanted to develop his part.

"Mickey was driving," he said, as if remembering. "So, at the top of the slope, at the roundabout, his eyes would have been looking right, looking for a gap in the traffic. Only I was still keeping obs on the van. I can tell you this. it didn't stop. If Jerry Garage got out, it would have had to be while it was moving, so yes, he might have incurred injuries. And yes, when we came out of the roundabout, heading down the slope back on to the motorway, we wouldn't have noticed a body on the grass, to the left. We were eyes forward."

"If there's even a chance - " Gibson began.

"If there is," Terry said, "I can use facial recognition to find which hospital he went into. I can tell you this. He wasn't using his own name. I've been through all the registrations and no one called 'Jerry Garage' arrived at a Hospital Reception that day."

"Well, of course not," Caulfield agreed. "That isn't his real name, is it?"

Mickey nodded. He knew that. The man had more than one passport.

He had worked with him.

On assignment (and undercover).

Gibson said: "Richard, you've been really helpful. We won't detain you longer."

"You have other things to investigate?" Caulfield asked nosily.

"Sure, a suspicious company called 'Henshykan'," Mickey said, ready to sign off.

Timely. The door burst open and Inspector de Angelis came rushing in.

When he saw the open laptop, he paused.

"If I'm interrupting - " he smapped.

"Not at all," the Captain reassured him. "Come in, Inspector, We're just finishing. Thanks again, Richard."

There was a click on the line, and the image disappeared.

"Really, I'm here to see Terry," the policeman said, apologising to the Captain. "Terry, do you have the map?"

Terry pulled a manila envelope off the desk. He opened it and took out a piece of paper.

It was a map, seemingly of countryside, and there were hardly any roads or buildings marked.

"Right," the policeman said, taking Terry for granted. "I now have all the information I need to mount an operation."

Gibson, trying hard not to exchange dubious glances with Mickey, merely asked: "What kind of 'operation' is that?"

"Maybe you need my assistance?" Mickey suggested gently.

"Stand down, Something," he was told. "It's time for Uniform. We'll be moving in at dawn."

Mickey said, still delving: "You must have some solid information, Dee."

"This is all I need," the Inspector said, waving the map. "Thank you, Gentlemen. I bid you Good Evening."

And he was gone.

Gibson looked reproachfully at Terry. "What did you give him? What does he think he's got?

Terry shrugged. "A Treasure Map, obviously. Look, I can't be held responsible with what people do with my info."

"What have you done?"

Terry tried to explain.

The Inspector had come to Terry and asked him if he could trace the mobile phones of the people on the minibus.

After all, every attendee at the event had signed in, putting their name and phone number, plus, email address, on a sheet of paper. Terry had got hold of a copy, and had routinely tried all the numbers. Not one of them was still connected.

The Police Inspector had arrived at Terry's office and asked: "Could you discover where they were when they failed?"

Terry tried to explain.

Sure, each of the victims might have been making calls while they were on the buss, maybe while the kidnapping had started. Perhaps the kidnappers had told the people to 'switch off their phones', but that wouldn't disguise their position: it was perfectly possible to work out a location even when a mobile was seemingly 'off'.

No, it was worse that that. For all the phones to be undiscoverable, then each person must have opened their handset and taken the battery out. (Or maybe the kidnappers did that for them. Possible. Kidnappers might have gathered up all the phones.)

But - the Inspector was relying on luck.

Just identify the last location each phone was 'alive', he urged, and plot it on a map.

Terry pulled out a duplicate of the document he handed to the policeman.

It showed a line of red dots, some overlapping, running along an isolated country road.

Terry said: "The Inspector is guessing that the phones were disabled shortly before they reached their destination. So, he's looking at this piece of map and saying to himself, 'Where is the nearest farm from that last point?' See?"

The assumption being that if the minibus had turned off the road, then the dots would turn abruptly left or right, as if making entrance into a farm. The fact that they were all in a line meant that they hadn't made their final destination yet.

Gibson said: "Okay, we see buildings along the road. Which is the likely one?"

Terry tapped the sheet.

"That one alongside the red dots is Harper Hay Farm," he said. "A huge barn, good for storing a stolen minibus. But no, the red dots are still running at this point, so it can't be them. The next building, after the red dots have finished, is Ritter's Farm. A good distance along, plenty of room to pull in, but no outbuildings at all. Where would you hide the minibus? Then, next, it's Nieman Jones's Farm."

"A possibility?" Mickey asked, thinking the whole thing was a far-fetched stretch.

Terry nodded. "Possible," he agreed.

Mr Gibson was shifting uncomfortably in his seat.

"All of this is only ever a slim likelihood if there was planning aforethought," he said. "But every bit of information we have accumulated so far, makes it seem a much more spontaneous happening. Who knew the men from the Developers were going to suggest a trip out into the countryside? So who had time to arrange a place to harbour prisoners?"

"And even if a journey had been mooted previously," Terry pointed out, "who knew what direction they would go in?"

"It's worse than that," Mickey agreed. "The people from the meeting clambered onto the minibus and set off. I saw them. So, where did the kidnappers come from? Were they following? When did they get on board?"

"You were following," Gibson pointed out, "for all but the smallest bit of the journey."

"Until the vehicle disappeared," Terry agreed. "But that could mean only one thing - "

"The 'kidnappers' had actualy got onto the bus as 'protesters' from the meeting," Mickey said slowly.

"Infiltrators," the Captain agreed.

Mickey sighed. "What we're saying is that we don't know 'How' the crime was done."

"Or 'Why', do we?" Gibson finished.

"We know one thing," Terry suggested slyly. "If the Inspector thinks he knows what he's doing, then my money says he's wrong. I'm willing to bet ten pounds that he if leads a raid on an isolated farmhouse, it will most probably be the wrong one!"

Chapter SEVEN: A ride on the tram

The next morning, Mickey got up early and went looking for the other minibus, the one 'in the garage for repairs'.

Mickey was annoyed.

Either the Inspector was right and he would come crash banging into a farmyard with his special forces and discover a minibus hidden within a barn, with more than a dozen dishevelled hostages looking sorry for themselves. Or Terry was right and, despite all the noise and fury, there would be nothing there.

Not there. But somewhere, Mickey was thinking.

One empty barn didn't prove anything. The kidnappers could have moved the sufferers anywhere by now. They could be captive in an old warehouse in Manchester, maybe, or on a boat, moored somewhere far down the Manchester Ship Canal, nearer the sea.

That didn't bear thinking about. There were just too many possibilities.

On the other hand, perhaps there was one problem that could be solved. The fourth minibus. Was it being repaired - right now - and had it been there all week and all weekend, which meant it couldn't have been used on Saturday?

Surprisingly, the school was happy to relay the name of the garage, and the address.

Mickey looked it up on his map and was pleased to see he could get there by tram.

In fact, that was the easy way.

Trams had spread out around Manchester, in the last few years, but the routes were still varied and idiosyncratic, depending on existing train lines or desperate need. One priority had been to provide an easy way for shoppers to get from the centre of the city out to The Irwell Centre. It was one of the biggest leisure destinations in Europe, but mostly it relied on people having cars or being willing to take a bus.

The new tram line was reliable, comfortable and frequent. If it could accommodate people with their bags of booty, then it was good for business, and business was what the Irwell Centre was all about.

So, that was the 'end of the line', but that particular route wended its way past Manchester United's football ground, and through Irwell Park, which sounds bucolic, but since Victorian times had been the centre of industry and engineering in the North West of England. It had been cleaned up a lot since then, and most of the new buildings were warehouses and distribution centres, rather than the kind of metal-bending enterprises that could make cars or aircraft. Still, in between the hangers were some smaller units.

One such was called 'Gary's Garage', apparently, and, conveniently for Mickey, was a mere twenty yards from a tram stop.

Mickey took a bus from his home in North Salford, straight into the city centre. Then he hopped on the first tram that came along, heading for Cornbrook, a sort of interchange. Many of the trams going through were aiming for Salford Quays, the BBC or the town of Eccles, but the Irwell Centre line was like a spur off this route and he waited patiently for the Shopping Special.

Sure enough it took him past the famous football ground, then the War Museum and the start of the industrial buildings.

A landmark was the old Irwell Park Hotel, a massive square block of brick Victoriana that had served its purpose, and was no longer in use. The steady stream of buyers and traders had eased off, and no longer required such accommodation.

The Hotel was on the left-hand side of the road, the garage was on the right.

The first door opened into a shed full of tyres.

"Next door," a young man shouted.

The next door led into a dim and shadowy cavern with an assortment of cars, some in pieces, some with their bonnets up.

"Can I help you?" a greasy man said, from under a bonnet.

"I'm looking for a minibus," Mickey informed him.

"It's behind you."

Mickey turned. A minibus - a school minibus, with the Academy flash on the side - was six feet in the air, on a hoist.

"We've checked the brakes," the man announced. "It's good to go."

"Are you Gary?" Mickey asked.

The man suddenly got interested. He put down whatever he was doing and came over, wiping his hands on a rag.

"Are you from the school?" he asked, suspiciously.

"No, I'm helping the police with their enquiries."

"I thought so," he said. "The school told me the Games Teacher was coming to pick it up, and you're not him. So, no, I'm not Gary. That was my Dad. He helped found the business in 1934, with his Dad. I grew up to take it over. What's your profession?"

"Mostly, I just ask annoying questions," Mickey admitted wryly. "Like, was it just the brakes that needed fixing?"

The man laughed. "All right," he said. "Call me Alan, and I'll tell you the story."

He indicated two fold-up chairs by the door. They were made of green canvas and hold holes in the arms for drinks.

Alan sat down and said: "That bus was assembled in England, but it's made of parts from all over the world. The doors come from France and the chassis from Germany. But the engine is from Japan. Now, the symptons were spluttering and hesitation while starting up, so we diagnosed it as a fault in the drive chain. We tried all the regular suppliers and they didn't have the right one in stock. They had to order a new one. Normally, a delivery of parts arrives on a ship every six weeks, but we were lucky: that ship had already sailed. We were expecting it in half the time. Unfortunately, a tanker broke down in the Suez Canal and everything got held up. It doesn't happen very often, but it happened to us. We've been waiting and waiting and repairs have been stalled."

"You tell a good story," Mickey told him. "But my question is: could someone have borrowed this bus last Saturday?"

"Hardly. The top's off the engine, and I told you - the drive chain was bust. It couldn't move anywhere until yesterday."

Mickey sighed. Okay, that was definite.

So where did the bus he saw Saturday come from? Mickey was starting to doubt his own memory. He saw an 'Academy' minibus, didn't he? He stood next to it and chatted to the driver, didn't he? It happened, didn't it?

Alan said: "Look, the school has got four buses, right? There's A, B, C and D. This one is C. Maybe you need to talk to Doug, the Games Teacher. It's his favourite vehicle. Two of the seats at the back have been taken out, so there's room for games kit."

Mickey nodded his head. I need to talk to somebody, he was thinking.

Alan consulted his watch. "I've told him the bus is finished and ready to be collected. Doug will be here in - oh, about half an hour. I would offer you a cup of tea, but our cups are cracked and dirty. If you don't want to catch anything, you could go over the road to one of the shops there and get a coffee. There's a street next to the Hotel, and there's a line of shops. You get a choice - one cafe, and two sandwich shops. If you get a takeaway coffee, you could get one for me too. I like it frothy, real milk. None of that nut stuff."

Mickey stood up. He could do that, he was thinking. He felt a bit unsteady on his feet, like the world was wobbling and uncertain, but coffee, yes, that was a thing. He could hold on to that idea.

Alan's directions were perfectly fine.

Mickey emerged into the sunshine, turned left, crossed the road and the tram track and found a parade of shops in the small street on the right of the Hotel. He was tempted by the smell of burning bacon, and went into the nearest takeaway food shop. They sold him a bacon barm, a plain white roll, and let him sit on a sort of bar stool, looking out the window onto the road while he ate it.

Then he picked up two coffees in heatproof paper cups and strolled back across the main road.

Doug, the guy from school, was already there.

"I know you," Mickey told him.

He was a black man.

He was the same guy who had been standing next to the minibus in the church car park on Saturday afternoon.

So why wasn't he kidnapped?

Why wasn't he being held prisoner right now?

For one moment, the man looked as if he was about to panic and run, then sanity got the better of him.

He accepted one of the coffees and sat in one of the green chairs.

Alan said: "Sure, I'll got and get my own coffee, then," and left them alone together.

Mickey sat down and said: "I hear this is Bus C."

"That's right," Doug told him. "I had 'D' on Saturday. No mystery. I have the keys to the school. I went over and picked up the nearest bus in the morning and drove it to the church. I was asked to bring a vehicle and be on standby."

"Who asked you?"

"Paolo."

Mickey sipped his coffee, thoughtfully.

Who?

And why. Why would this person think that they would need transport? Was it planned. then, after all?

"I thought the trip to 'see the development south of Stockport' was a spontaneous thing," he mused.

"Maybe," Doug said. "I don't know. But Paolo was one of the organisers. He arranged for all the speakers to come - the MP, the

Councillors and the Mayor. And he arranged for me. And the vehicle. So, No. It was more than spontaneous."

"Tell me more about him."

"Paolo McCully. You must have seen him. He was sitting on the right, at the top table. A short, squat guy. Used to work around here, I think, in the Park. A machine grinder, I think he says. Many years. A Union man. Very left wing."

Mickey hadn't got as far as going in to the Church. He hadn't seen the table of VIPs.

"Did he get kidnapped?" he asked.

Doug looked confused. "I don't know about this 'kidnap' stuff," he said, sipping his coffee. "I've heard about it, but it makes no sense to me. The people got on my minibus, I drove them south and dropped them off. Then I came home."

"You didn't get kidnapped?" Mickey said.

"I came home. I put the minibus back in its slot, (Minibus D), and I went home to watch the football."

"Where?" Mickey gasped. "Where did you unload them?"

"Harper Hay Farm."

Mickey was struggling.

He had looked at Terry's map, and that particular building was past the place where all the phones went dead.

"You must have turned around," Mickey said.

"Sure, I did," the driver said. "I missed the turning. So, we went along until we came to a Lay-by. It was a big parking place, with a van selling greasy hot dogs. I drove past that van, came out at the far exit, turned right, back on ourselves, and found the farm entrance again."

"The kidnappers told you to do that?"

"Paolo told me. He was giving directions."

Doug finished his coffee and looked stern. He was being as helpful as he could, but he thought Mickey wasn't hearing him.

"I don't know who got kidnapped," he said. "I drove the bus. I was asked to do it, and I did it. But then, you must have seen what happened - you were following us. You must have seen me heading back up to Salford."

Mickey was stunned.

No, he saw the minibus had disappeared. He didn't notice a vehicle with an 'Academy' flash going past him later, back to the city.

Mickey thought about what he had been told before.

Somebody said that the police had called in at every farm along that road and looked in every barn. They found nothing.

Then he was thinking about the Inspector.

The police guy was raiding a farm, expecting to see a kidnapped minibus, one that had somehow been missed in the first visits. But there wasn't one.

There never had been.

But would he find the people?

Eighteen souls had gone out from the church that afternoon, and all but one had never been seen again.

Up to now.

Mickey was talking to the one 'survivor'.

So far.

Chapter EIGHT: People in glass houses

The message from Captain Gibson asked Mickey to meet him at Global City, the media destination by the river.

It was a while later, and Mickey was on a tram home by then, but that didn't matter. He could get off at Cornbrook and hop on a tram heading up the other line to Eccles, or maybe in to Global City. That was a spur, a minor diversion on the Eccles route, but so many media people needed to get to Global the tram company sent extra vehicles just for them, all through the day.

Mickey was intrigued. What could be so important that Gibson needed his company? There was a media person involved? What would the boss of an anti-terrorism Unit want with a journalist? Mickey was about to find out.

The tram stop at Global was right outside the BBC, with ITV, the independent television broadcaster, on the right, and a whole series of contractors and programme makers in the buildings behind. Oh, and there was the University, Salford University School of Media Studies. They were all grouped around the large and airy piazza. On the ground floors of these high-rise buildings there were bars and restaurants, delis and bistros. A choice of places to eat.

Gibson wasn't inside any of these.

He was out on the grass. In a greenhouse.

Blame Covid.

During the few years when the country went into regular lockdowns, and ordinary people were forbidden to mix and socialise, several of the bars in the area came up with the idea of erecting tents, sheds and glass houses where people in 'bubbles' would be allowed to meet without hindrance. It was a bright idea, popular, and even though the threat of the pandemic had receded, drinkers and customers still enjoyed the privacy offered by these 'temporary' little houses.

Maybe Mr Gibson, didn't want to be overheard.

Why not? He was shouting.

"That's 'News', isn't it?" he was saying, trying to get a message through to the media man.

The man shook his head, sadly. He didn't agree with the older man.

Unfortunately for the Captain, this scruffy fellow, in jeans and ripped t-shirt, held all the cards. He was the one making decisions.

"He's an Editor," Gibson said to Mickey, not waiting for introductions or the niceties. "His name is Diego."

"I'm trying to explain - " the laid-back youngster said quietly. "In every 'magazine' type programme, we have a Lead, the well-known name, who asks all the questions, and a Producer, who is responsible for keeping the show on air - "

"And an Editor," Gibson said gruffly, not politely, "who actually makes the choices of which items to feature."

Mickey tried to say something, but he wasnt allowed an edge in.

"Eighteen people," the Captain said, obviously trying to contain his irritation. "Disappeared - and you don't think that's important!"

"Important for friends and family - " the young man said, as though he was starting to agree.

"Who haven't heard from them. Not one. No communication," the Captain reiterated. "What? You think they're on holiday?"

The young man spread his hands, and raised his shoulders, as if there was no answer to that question.

Luckily, the confrontation was interrupted.

A young man in a waistcoat was tapping on the glass.

He politely slid back the door and deposited a tray on the table. A beer for Gibson and something else for young Diego.

An ice cream sundae, chocolate flavour.

"Anything for you, sir?" he asked Mickey.

"Coffee."

The waiter nodded and disappeared.

"Where were we?" Gibson said, sipping his ice cold brew.

"Going around the houses?" Mickey suggested.

He sympathised. He didn't understand the way the Media worked, either. Maybe if a child had vanished, one child, it would have been a big story. But eighteen grown men and women, somehow that didn't hit a nerve.

Who cared?

Diego had a long-handled spoon in his paw and was lapping up the ice cream. Why not? It was another warm day, the sun was shining, and it was, of course, hotter inside the glasshouse than out.

Mickey said: "Is it something to do with the building company, the developers? Is that the reason you can't mention what happened on the radio? Is there an Embargo? A Court Order, maybe? Are you worried about being sued?"

The kid looked genuinely baffled. No, he didn't think that was it.

Mickey had a brainwave.

"Is it because you've got no one to interview?" he suggested. "The hostages are all incommunicado, and there's no grieving relatives that have come forward. If we could provide that - a weeping wife missing her husband, a handsome young man missing his fiancee - would that tip the balance? Could you make that one of your features then?"

Diego nodded, thinking about it. That would help.

But there was something else.

"Look, let's be serious," he said, taking a break between mouthfuls, "you had the Mayor and the MP at your meeting. Several local Councillors, you say. But strangely, none of them were a target. Instead, twenty local people were grabbed, or snatched, or made off with, but we don't know any of them. We haven't heard of them. They're not famous. Why would the public care?"

"Your listeners - " Mickey started, then stopped, flabbergasted.

"Yes, Mickey," the Captain said, putting it into words, "our friend here is saying that the people who disappeared are nobodies. They're human beings, warm, living bodies, but not one is a famous name. They've gone? The listeners don't care!"

"I just don't see an angle!" Diego confessed. "Where's the warmth? The drama? You want to publicise some building project, a high-rise block of apartments - it's all bricks and windows. Nobody would listen to a story of cement."

Mickey was not a violent man, usually, but at that point he was willing to punch the guy.

Luckily there was another arrival.

It was the police Inspector.

He pulled back the glass door and left it open behind him, plumping himself down on a seat, gratefully.

"Your office said I would find you here," he said, addressing the Captain.

Mickey wanted to ask his pal Dee about the raid on the farm, but Inspector de Angelis was having none of it.

"We've found the red sports car," he announced.

"Where was it?"

"Up a tree."

The cop said: "There's a long hill, going round a bend and up into the forest. (You may remeber it, Mickey.) Well, the sports car was coming back, heading downhill. It must have been going at quite a speed. It missed the turning, went through the barrier and headed out into open space, at tree top height. Unfortunately there was a tree in the way. It smashed into the branches and became stuck. It's been there for days. According to the Medics on the scene, the two people inside probably didn't die immediately."

"But they didn't call for help?" Mickey asked, stunned.

"They couldn't move. Their arms and legs were trapped. You can't exactly call for help from the top of a tree."

Gibson said to the media fellow: "That good enough for you? That's a story!"

"Too gory," the young man said decisively. "Our audience wouldn't like that."

He went back to his ice cream.

He hadn't been persuaded and the Inspector, although he had only just arrived, grasped the situation.

"You're not putting us at the top of your News Bulletin?" he asked. "Eighteen people disappeared - "

"Sixteen," the kid said, "if you're counting out two men in a sports car."

"Fifteen," Mickey said. "The minibus driver is home and accounted for. With his vehicle."

The Inspector shook his head sadly, as if the whole investigation was collapsing in front of his eyes.

Mickey said to him: "What about your raid on the farm?"

"It was a bust," the cop said. "We found no minibus - but then, your story explains that - and no sign of people. Not any. None."

"Which farm did you go to, eventually?"

"Harper Hay Farm. I just had a hunch, a feeling in my gut."

Mickey said: "You figured the minibus might have turned around?" When Dee nodded, Mickey added: "That's what I was told."

Diego, the Editor, had finished his sundae and was looking around, as if ready to leave.

"So, gentlemen," he said, as if slightly sad, "you have nothing for me. Maybe if there was something definite - "

"Like a Ransom Note?" the Inspector suggested.

"Exactly," the media man said, thinking about it.

"Then it's good I have one here," the cop replied.

He reached into an inside pocket and drew out a piece of white paper, with a small amount of printing at the top.

"You can touch it," he said, passing it around. "It's been dusted for prints and so on."

Captain Gibson was interested. "It's asking for a million dollars to 'release the prisoners'. That's it?"

"That tells us a lot," Mickey said. "If it was British gangsters, they'd be asking for a million pounds. Right? If they were Eastern Europeans, it would be Euros, maybe. But dollars? No, they must be international criminals."

"Why?" Gibson asked them all. "Who are they trying to threaten?"

"They want the development company to pay it," the policeman said. "It's to embarrass them, inconvenience them. Bring bad publicity and maybe slow up the whole building project. It doesn't affect the company itself - the people aren't employees - but it would reflect on the money men if they just ignored this demand. They don't want to appear uncaring."

Mickey was a little confused about that. If he was the one holding hostages, why would it matter who paid? Salford Council?

Besides., Mickey knew something the others didn't. Doug the driver had told him the 'hostages' disembarked from the coach in an orderly manner, but no one was threatening them. So who were the 'kidnappers' who sent the note?

What if it was they themselves who did it? What if it had come from Paolo McCully, to extort the development company?

The Inspector went on: "The Company aren't going to want to pay, of course. They are already trying to distance themselves from the whole campaign, and everyone in it. Such as, well, we have a problem with the two guys in the sports car. We were told that they introduced themselves at the meeting as an architect and a landscape gardener. Turns out that's true. They had identification on them, and we've managed to trace them back to their addresses and business details. However, Henshykan is saying that they didn't hire them and didn't ask them to go to the Public Meeting."

Mickey had to start thinking about that. Anybody could have hired them. If you wanted two 'men in suits', people who knew enough about buildings and construction to make it believable if they were asked a question -

Diego stood up and dusted himself down. He wasn't looking his best. The extreme heat had made him sweat, a lot.

"All right, I'll give it a shot," he said. "I'll go and talk to my Manager and see if it can be slotted into the Evening News bulletin."

"We'd all be very grateful," Captain Gibson told him, trying not to sound sarcastic.

"There's going to be more," the Inspector promised him. "Tell him that. It's a fast moving situation now."

"Her."

The media man slid out from behind the table and out of the greenhouse. As he did so, the Captain's phone rang.

"It's Terry," he announced, and put it to his ear. "I see. I see, Yes, yes."

He looked around as he cut the connection. There was an interested look in his eye.

"The Unit has had a call from Mr Caulfield," he said slowly. "It's for you, Mickey. He wants to talk to you, when you've got time."

Me? Mickey was thinking.

What possible item of interest would cause the ex-Deputy Director to get in touch with him, all the way from Australia?

It's not as though they were friends.

Chapter NINE: Hospital beds

"Who is the Man in the Mask?" Terry joked.

Mickey was uncomfortable.

You tell me, he was thinking to himself. I don't know what I'm doing in this hospital.

They were both sitting in uncomfortable chairs next to a bed, in a side ward of the biggest hospital in South Manchester. It was famous for its plastic surgery. In the bed was a man wrapped in bandages. His entire face was covered.

He was asleep.

"You tracked him down?" Mickey asked the computer geek.

"You'd be surprised," Terry said, starting a lecture, "how many people arrive in hospital with no identification. The National Health Service doesn't turn anyone away, so the patient starts treatment and someone in the Admin Department is left to try and work out who they're dealing with. Mainly, they want to find out if they've got any relatives, family at home - a place they can call 'home', even."

"So they can be chucked out, eventually?"

"It's called 'Bed Blocking'," Terry agreed. "You'd be surprised how many people get cured from whatever is troubling them, only to be stuck in a hospital bed for months, even years. It's a national scandal. Yes, the hospital wants to discharge him - "

"Hello, Mickey," the body said.

The voice was raspy and barely audible, but the inflections were recognisable.

It was Jerry Garage.

"I was in the car behind you," Mickey said briefly, not bothering with niceties. "I saw the van blow up. I thought you were inside."

"No such luck," the politician croaked. "Ian Bann, the younger, was determined to murder his Dad - and himself - but he had no grudge against me. He executed a maneouvre, up off the road and onto a roundabout, then pushed me out the door as he drove back down onto the motorway. I hit the grass, bounced, and was out cold for hours until someone spotted my body."

Mickey felt bad.

That meant HE didn't spot him, either. He was in the car, and must have driven past the exited Mr Garage, not noticing.

"You seem to have a good memory," Mickey observed.

"Not really," Jerry said, "but I've had plenty of time to think about it. I was in a coma for several weeks - "

"And then treatment - "

"The whole of my face was crushed. Both cheekbones," he added. "They had to rebuild my beautiful visage."

Mickey couldn't suppress a grin.

Mr Garage liked to have his name pronounced the American way - 'Gah-Raj'.

'Mr 'Gah-Raj' with a wonderful visage'. That rhymed!

"I'm glad to see you're alive," Mickey said. He'd always had a grudging respect for the man he had spied on.

"You and me both! But how did you find me?"

"That was my job," Terry admitted. "I looked for your name, but you hadn't checked in, using the usual procedures. You were unconscious when they brought you in, and then in a coma? No wonder there was no record of an admittance around the date."

Jerry nodded his head, getting the idea, but it felt painful, so he stopped doing it.

Terry said: "Then I tried facial recognition, but you've been wrapped in bandages for weeks, so nothing showed up. It was only when your associates started trying to hide where you were, that your name popped up. We have surveillance on your little Party, and everything they do is monitored. The fact they started visiting this hospital - "

"And gave me a fake name? A person who didn't exist? Yeah, I can see how it raised flags."

Mr Garage didn't seem upset. He trusted the two visitors. Terry he recognised as the man who used to organise the PA system at his rallies, and Mickey was a person he worked closely with, for several months. He had no idea either of them had been been brought in by Captain Gibson, as part of the Unit's ongoing investigations into smaller political parties.

"Anyway, boys," he said patronisingly, "you've arrived at an auspicious moment. Today's the day the bandages come off."

Mickey nodded, giving Terry a look. It wasn't a coincidence, he knew. Nothing was, with Terry.

"Maybe you've got time for a coffee," Jerry suggested.

"They have not," a nurse said, bustling in. "The doctor is on his way."

Several doctors. And Nurses. And Trainees. They all wanted to see the result of so much intensive treatment.

They sat Mr Garage up in bed and several nurses wielded scissors, approaching from different directions.

"Gently," the chief Doctor urged, being cautious. "There's no hurry. Take your time."

The bandages were peeled away, layer upon layer, until a full face was revealed. Then other nurses moved in, each holding a sponge or wet flannel. They carefully, carefully wiped the reconstructed cheekbones, forehead and chin.

The medics broke out into spontaneous applause, impressed by the detailed work.

Terry's phone rang.

He moved to the back of the ward to take the call, avoiding the disapproving glances.

Mickey joined him.

"He looks different," Mickey hissed.

Terry was quietly listening, but Mickey just couldn't help say his thoughts out loud.

"He can't just go back into business like that," Mickey mumbled. "He can't re-appear and take up the reins. People will say it isn't him. The stand-in's have done such a good job of being him, the voters are convinced that nothing abnormal has happened. Jerry can't chuck out people who look like him without having to admit he's been away and they aren't him."

"He's caused his own dilemma," Terry agreed.

But Terry knew more.

He knew that Jerry Garage hadn't been sleeping quietly for months. He had a contract with The Daily Pitch, a horrible newspaper, to write a weekly column, full of vitriol and spleen. He had been doing that - the genuine Jerry. He hadn't trusted any minions to write with his tone and attitudes. Also, he had been writing speeches that the actors spouted, on his behalf.

And the internet. When comments and libels were bounced around social media, it all came from this man, from this hospital bed.

But Mickey was right, Terry appreciated. What 'handover' could there possibly be, that wouldn't undermine his image?

"On the plus side," Terry noted, "he's actually quite handsome now."

"But if anyone wants to make a film of Jerry's life," Mickey said seriously, "they won't be able to use this version."

That might have been enough of a problem for one day, but Terry had been called with more news.

"They want you downstairs, Mickey," he said, and his voice was serious.

Mickey was concerned, but he saw that Jerry Garage was getting enough attention from the medics to keep him busy, so he allowed Terry to lead him outside and into the busy corridor. They approached the lifts.

"How far downstairs?" Mickey said, jocularly.

"All the way," Terry said, not laughing.

They got into the lift and Terry pressed the button for the basement.

Mickey saw that it was labelled 'Mortuary'.

He didn't say anything. He trusted Terry, and Terry had been given information. Terry would check it, maybe, or, at least, think about it. He wouldn't take Mickey on a wild goose chase. Whatever the need, it would be real.

"What do they want me to do?" he asked.

"Identify a body."

They came out into a corridor. It was cooler here, as if the central heating wasn't needed.

A side door went off into the underground car park but a sign on the wall said 'Mortuary' and they followed that.

"I'm sorry, Mickey," Terry sad, his voice practically a whisper.

Someone had died? Mickey was thinking. He'd had no notification! Shouldn't he have been contacted directly?

Maybe there was some doubt. Maybe no one was certain and they were relying on Mickey - as if Mickey was the only person who could confirm the identity of the deceased. But why? Was it another uncertainty, like when Jerry Garage was admitted?

They turned left through double doors and a doctor was standing there in green scrubs.

"Thanks for coming," he said directly to Mickey. "This won't be pleasant and you will need to prepare yourself."

Now Mickey was really scared. His heart was racing, and he felt a sweat, despite the low temperature in the area.

The medic opened a door and led the pair into another room.

There was a body on a slab, covered in a thin white sheet.

Mickey stared hard, but could tell nothing from the outline, or the length of the person. Who could it possibly be?

The man in green went to the head end and took hold of an edge of the sheet.

"Ready? he asked and Mickey nodded.

It was Billy Budman.

He was dead, no doubt about it. There were ugly scars on his face and it looked like his hair was matted over injuries.

The doctor said: "Police pulled his body out of the Blaneyboar Reservoir. He had drifted into the outlet, which is probably how he got a little mashed up. We've done preliminary examinations and we don't think he drowned. He died elsewhere."

"He was dumped?" Mickey said, his anger flashing.

Who? Who could have done such a thing to his old pal, his mate from Army days?

"And his wheelchair," the doctor said, musing. "He was in his chair. It's a bit incongruous."

Mickey felt his blood pressure soar. He was about to explode.

He turned away. It wasn't the doctor's fault. There was no point in shouting at him. But still -

Mickey was baffled. He had started to believe that Doug the driver was right and he had dropped off all the people in his minibus at a farm. At that point they were all cheerful and well. Then, when the bus was gone, they made some other arrangement and went somewhere else, where they could stay - out of sight - and not be found. They were just planning to hide out for a week, maybe more.

But nobody was expected to die!

What on Earth had gone wrong that Billy Bud had died? An argument? A falling out? Had they been fighting?

If he had been alone, Mickey knew full well that he would have smashed his fist into a wall.. He was fighting mad. He was frustrated. He was full of anger and fear, but there was nowhere for the feelings to go. Maybe later -

Terry was helpless. He had never been in the Army, never served. He had no experience of the kinds of bonds that grown men forge under fire. He couldn't begin to imagine the kinds of thoughts that Mickey was having.

But he stood by, and was happy to escort his colleague out of the room.

He knew one thing. Mickey wouldn't let it go. Here was another mystery that he would want to solve, need to solve.

He wouldn't stop until he had answers.

They walked slowly back towards the lift. What now?

Terry said, simply suggesting: "Shall we go back and see if we can talk to Mr Garage?"

Mickey was breathing heavily, his breath rasping, He nodded. What else could they do? There was nothing that Mickey could do right now for his pal Billy. The door was closed. The kid was gone.

Mickey found himself grinding his teeth. Someone was going to have to pay! he was thinking.

They went back up in the lift and came out into an empty corridor. There was no one around.

Walking along to Jerry Garage's room, they found a single policeman standing outside.

The bed was bare.

The cop said: "We were asked to clear the area and the patient was escorted out of the building."

"Is he well enough?" Terry gasped.

The cop shrugged. That was none of his business. Really, he didn't care.

He said: "His associates came and took him away. Whoever he was, he must have been a very important person."

'Whoever'?

Mickey gasped, Of course! Mr Garage had a new face. Even the policeman - who might have been a supporter of Jerry and his party -

didn't recognise him. The cop was there, and Jerry was assisted to walk right past him.

This was the way of the future, Mickey realised.

The real Jerry Garage was a new face in British politics!

Chapter TEN: Into the woods (again)

The next day, Mickey was still seething.

For once, he wasn't about to be fobbed off with stories and lies. He wanted answers!

He got into his car, and drove out into the country, heading to the south of Stockport.

The road he had taken the previous Saturday wasn't hard to find, and looked exactly the same. It had hedges on either side, lots of trees visible, and was undulating, up and down hills. For a moment, he thought of seeking out that bend where the men in suits had come off in their bright, new red sports car. Then decided against it - those people weren't his priority.

The residents were, the the ones who had climbed into the school minibus, unaware they were being set up. A jaunt into the countryside would be turned into a fake kidnapping, and for why? To attract publicity? Sympathy? Highlight their concerns about the planning issues of losing their local shops?

Suddenly, it didn't seem funny anymore. A modest lark had turned into murder, maybe, and the deceased was Mickey's pal.

What happened? he mused. How could it have ended in death? What could possibly have gone wrong?

And who was to blame?

The first stop wasn't a big decision.

Doug the driver had said that he dropped off the party at Harper Hay Farm, so that was where Mickey went first.

The turning was clearly marked, with a sign showing the name. There was no owner mentioned, though. No phone number.

There was a five bar gate just off the road, but it was open.

The way in was a dirt track, and not even tarmaced. It was uneven, and Mickey's car bounced around. He tried to avoid the potholes, but it wasn't possible. It's wide enough for a tractor, he was thinking. Or a minibus. One Way. No room for passing.

The drive ended at a substantial farmhouse building, and there were barns and maybe stables on either side.

Still, no back road. Behind the house was a line of trees that smothered a hill, rising up. No tracks, no roads.

One way in and one way out. A cul-de-sac, as they might say in Salford.

But, from the main road to the farm it was remarkably flat, with extensive fields on either side. Is this where it got its name, this place? It looked like there was grass growing, and perhaps the barn was there for the hay bales to be stored.

Mickey didn't really understand farming. He looked around for the cows and sheep, but there weren't any.

No other vehicles, so he could park right outside the front door, then jump out and bang loudly on an antique knocker.

Silence.

Mickey, wound up and frustrated, wanted to do something, anything.

He knew that if a person had answered that knock and opened the door, he would have probably leapt on them. Still -

He heard a noise.

It sounded like talking, and was coming from an open building off to the right. A stable?

Mickey wasn't about to slow down, to take it easy. He had no intention of being cautious.

He bounded through the open door, looking for trouble. Then he stopped.

A young kid, maybe six or seven years old, was sitting on a horse. The youngster was clearly having fun. He was laughing.

"Where's your Dad?" Mickey demanded roughly.

A face popped out from behind a wooden stall. A middle-aged, pot-bellied man had a rake in his hand.

"You the farmer?" Mickey snarled.

"No."

Micket deflated like a birthday balloon.

The man, worried about his kid, but happy to explain, told Mickey that he and his family had hired the farmhouse for the week.

"There is no farmer," he said. "This whole building is to rent."

Mickey was suspicious.

"There's fields out there," he said. "Somebody is growing the grass and cutting it down."

"Oh yeah, we've met the guy," the Dad said. "Max has taken a ride on his harvester. It's a lot of fun. But no, the guy lives further down the road. He rents these fields, he was telling us. It's an addition to his own acreage."

Mickey chewed over the information. This wasn't what he expected.

"When did you arrive?" he asked.

"Monday."

So, they wouldn't have seen a minibus arrive on Saturday afternoon, he was thinking. Darn.

"There's no car," he said, as if accusing the guy of something bad.

""My wife has gone into Stockport to do some shopping," the man explained. "Look, can I offer you a cup of tea?"

"Not right now. Mind if I have a look around?"

"Be my guest."

Mickey came out of the dim building and walked around the back of the farmhouse.

Rented? The building was rented? The fields were rented?

Sure, maybe he could ask the father if he had details of the owner, but would that help? If that person lived elsewhere, maybe they wouldn't be a witness to the arrival of Doug and his passengers.

But there was no road out! Mickey kept thinking. Just woods going up the hill -

He reached the exact rear of the buildings and saw something strange. A sign. A finger-post. It read, 'Right of Way'.

There was a path, snaking away through the trees. The narrowest kind of way, with a dirt floor and trees and bushes crowding out the passage on either side. Would the 'visitors' have walked up there?

Mickey had one thought: it wasn't really wide enough for a wheelchair. Could his pal Billy Bud have got up that slope?

There was no reason why Mickey could have thought that was a possibility, but right at that moment, he was clutching at straws.

He followed the path.

It snaked backwards and forwards, which helped the climb up the hill, but the trees were thick - a mix of old and new firs - and it wasn't possible to see what was ahead.

It was a warm day and Mickey was sweating freely. He had to take his jacket off and sling it over his arm.

I can't guess where this is going to come out, he was thinking. Would there be a clearing, a road, another path?

Mickey wasn't expecting a sign.

It read: 'Eco Forest Healing. Well-being for the whole family'.

He came out into a small clearing. There was a fire pit in the middle, with logs grouped around, for seating.

On each side, partly hidden amongst the trees, were a series of log cabins, rows of them, jumbled out of sight.

Mickey almost laughed.

'Well-being'? That's what I need, he was thinking.

But it didn't do Bill Budman much good!

A man was walking across the lawn swinging a bucket in his hand.

"I'm looking for people from Salford," Mickey said, loudly.

"Not me," the man said, smiling. "I'm from Australia. Also, I'm staff. I clean the rooms."

"Can I talk to the Manager?"

"If there was one," the muscley replied, laughing. "We don't work like that, I'm afraid."

"I don't understand - "

"Try this one," the man suggested. "This one here. 'Avalon 3'. I think that might be someone from your group."

Mickey followed the pointing finger.

The cabins weren't numbered, so there was no way of telling one from another. But the cleaning guy seemed to know.

Mickey went between trees and came to a porch. He was about to knock on the door but stopped.

He saw a hammock on the left, slowly swinging.

"Hello?" he said, trying not to be too threatning. "Hello?"

A face popped out over the canvas. A lady. A middle-aged lady.

"Do I know you?" she asked politely.

"Were you in Salford last Saturday? A meeting at the church by the park?"

"Certainly," she said. "Guilty as charged. Oh, wait. I do recognise you. You were standing by the minibus when we came out."

That's me, he was thinking. Guilty as charged.

"I'm a friend of Billy's. Have you seen him?"

"Oh, Billy. Such a shame. How is he now?"

Mickey was taken aback. Shouldn't SHE know? Didn't he die on these premises?

"Let me make you a cup of tea," she said, and clambered out of the hammock clumsily.

Mickey took a seat on the porch. After a while, the woman came back with two steaming mugs.

"I used to be a nurse," she said, regretfully. "I should have known there was something wrong. He had a turn shortly after we got here. He said something about 'medicine' but refused anyone's offer of going to get some from the town."

"Why would he do that?"

"He said he thought it might give us away."

"So what happened?" Mickey went on, prompting.

"He had a fit one night. We got him into Recovery position, and he came to quickly. But I was worried. We all agreed we should get him into hospital, and Paolo persuaded one of his pals to lend him a car, but Billy still refused to go. In the morning, Bill was unconscious again."

Or not breathing, Mickey was thinking. Would Paolo admit that, or do his best to keep their gang hidden?

"Anyway," the woman said, "some of the men got Billy into the back of the car and off they went. How is he? Is he better?"

She didn't know!

Mickey shrugged, not answering. There was no point in trying to make the woman face unpleasant facts.

"How can you drive a car off this site?" he enquired, as if he knew nothing, which he didn't.

"Oh, there's an access road on this side, which goes over the hill and down onto the other road into Stockport. We came up the path through the trees, like you did. but once here, it's easy getting in and out."

"And who's the 'pal' with the car?"

"Oh, one of the Trade Unionists. Don't you know this whole place was set up as a Recuperation Camp for Trade Union people? Paolo is up to his neck in the Trade Unions, always has been. But, hey - why so many questions? You a cop?"

Mickey grinned. Nothing like it, he said. But he was anxious about what happened to his friend Bill.

"I've told you as much as I know," she said. "Anyway, he's gone out of camp, and that makes about half now."

"People have left?"

"Drifted away. They want to see their families again, obviously. They wander off, just 'go for a walk', and disappear up the access road and down to the main road. There's a bus every hour. They can get back into Stockport, then a train or bus after that."

"When's this 'holiday' meant to end?"

"Oh, don't worry. We've got a plan. Paolo has organised another meeting this Saturday afternoon. He's found someone to provide transport, so we'll waltz into the meeting and who knows - someone might applaud our efforts."

Sure, if the fake 'kidnap' works and the campaign gets the ransom money, Mickey was thinking.

Then, he said out loud: "So, where is Paolo now? Perhaps I really should be speaking to him."

"No doubt," she agreed. "But you'll have a problem with that. A police car arrived about an our ago, and the busies loaded him in and whisked him away. If he gets a phone call, maybe he'll be able to tell us where he is and how he is."

"And if not?"

"Then good luck to him. The rest of us will be carrying on with the plan. So, we'll see you Saturday."

Mickey stood up.

He gathered his jacket, looking around the incredible, rustic camp, shaking his head at the unlikelihood of it all.

She said, quickly, "Oh, I didn't mean you have to go now. Don't you want to stay for the nightly barbecue?"

Mickey shook his head.

"Thanks, but I've got a car back down the hill by the farmhouse. I think I'll be making my way back home."

"Well, see you Saturday."

"Saturday," he agreed.

Chapter ELEVEN: The Mayor and the money men

"Thanks for coming, Mickey," the elected Mayor of Salford said to Mickey.

The Mayor was in his office in Salford's Civic Centre in Swinton. There was someone else there too.

"This is Councillor Derby," the Mayor said. "I'd like to emphasis the Councillor is not from my political party - "

"We're working together on this," Salem Derby said, for the benefit of the other two men present.

They were from Henshykan, they said.

One was an architect and one a Landscape Gardiner.

That made Mickey gasp. They were clones of the two people that were at the meeting on Saturday. Same suits, same haircuts. Same enthusiasm. The former pair had ended up in a tree, Mickey wanted to say. Beware, Gentlemen.

Instead, he said out loud: "Captain Gibson wanted me to come."

Mickey knew that the elected Mayor knew the Captain. They had worked together before. They trusted each other.

One of the suits said: "We were told you were working with a Police Inspector, and that you might know where the captives are."

Mickey gulped.

He hadn't told anyone he had even gone down that road!

Something stopped him then. He didn't want to admit anything to these two 'professionals'. He didn't trust them as far as he could throw them. Why would he? They were happily taking part in a plan to demolish the affordable shops in East Salford -

"It might be easier to talk," the Councillor said, acidly, "if we were here with someone rather higher up the scale that you two. No offense, but it seems that the Council is always being fobbed off with 'spokespersons' rather than Executives."

The architect looked taken aback. "We speak for the Company here," he said. "People in London - "

"Work on the Grand Plan, the vision," Derby said. "You, you're an architect. What's your role?"

"I'm taking Lead on Building Four," he said resentfully. "I really don't know who you expect."

"The owners!" the Councillor exploded. "The people who live in the Channel Islands."

The Gardener smiled. "The company is registered in Jersey," he explained. "But the 'owners' live in London."

"And would command more respect if they paid taxes in England," the Councillor noted.

"Let's all calm down," the elected Mayor said.

The Mayor, Sol Senate, was known to Mickey. In fact, Mickey had saved him from an assassin once. They respected each other.

Mr Senate had been elected Mayor, but Salford being Salford, absorbed that new opportunity when it arose in 2012, and carried on with a 'Ceremonial Mayor', who wore the gold chair and velvet cloak. Meanwhile, Mr Senate made the decisions.

He said: "The reason we're here is because we are in the process of agreeing a second meeting, this coming Saturday. Same venue, the church, and same invitation to all residents. Plus, you two employees of the Developers, to speak on their behalf."

"But," Councillor said, still irritated, "without the stonewalling and obfuscation this time. Things have moved on."

The architect was willing to be generous.

"Well, yes, things have moved on," he said. "We know a lot more about where the residents stand now. The letters and comments have come in, and we've seen the Petition. The Master Plan might not be affected, but we can stage delivery, perhaps."

The Councillor was about to blast again, but Mayor Senate waved him down.

"We've heard that you're planning to spread the building work over ten years, starting at the east side of the site," Sol said. "That isn't necessarily a good thing. That means a decade of building work, a nightmare for the people who move into the first blocks. They might have a nice view of the river on the east side, but the other side will be scaffolding and diggers, for years."

"The supermarket," Mickey said, suddenly picking up the implications, "is staying, right? But that means shoppers will be driving through dirt and dust in order to get to the Sangford's car park. Won't they be put off?"

The architect gave a very obvious look of 'Not my concern', and didn't even bother trying to excuse the plan.

"Let's talk about money," he suggested. "That's what you really want to hear. The whole scheme is budgeted at one billion pounds over the ten years. Our company is willing to offer the residents one million pounds in Section 106 payments."

Mickey knew what that meant. 'Section 106' was part of The Housing Act 1988. (He had come across this part when he was temporarily CEO of the Corsh Corporation, a local Development company.) The Developer was obliged to offer the local Council a sum of money - based on the cost of the development - that would go to help the local community, in some social way.

The Councillor was not impressed.

"Mr Mayor," he said. "This has happened before. The builders offer an impressive wedge of cash, in the hope that Planning Permission is waved through. Then, when building starts, they come back with some excuse about how they can't pay."

Mickey had heard about that too. Developers had invented a concept called 'normal profits'. If they didn't look like making an expected surplus, they would plead poverty. It was a wonderful fantasy land they lived in.

The architect said: "Then good job we are paying up front."

Mickey and Derby were surprised. It was left to the Mayor to explain.

"It seems we need a million pounds right now," he said. "Inspector de Angelis has been in and brought the ransom notes for us to look at. The kidnappers want the million - in cash - delivered to the meeting on Saturday."

Since Mickey knew that the 'kidnappers' might be the same people as the 'captives', it made sense to Mickey that they might be asking to see the cash at the community meeting. (Although, logically, they couldn't appear - 'free' - until the ransom was paid!)

Sol Senate said: "The Council can't find a million pounds in cash."

"We can," the architect said.

"It's like a temporary loan," Mayor Senate explained. "Even if the cash is handed over - to someone or other - we expect the Inspector and plain clothes police to be on hand to arrest the bad guys and get the money back."

"We hope so," the architect said. "There is no second million. If the first million disappears, then the 'Section 106' money goes."

"We'll try not to lose it," Mickey promised.

* * * * *

Four hours later, Mickey came walking around the corner into his road and saw Denise waiting for him.

"I've got some information," she said curtly.

She had a sheaf of papers in her hand.

So did Mickey.

"You'd better come in," he said.

They trailed into the kitchen and Mickey made a pot of coffee. His guest was happy with that, and refused food.

"You first," Mickey said, sitting opposite her.

"Well, the thing is," she started, "I talk to men for a living. Mainly they're drunk, but that's my fault. I encourage them to buy booze."

Mickey nodded. He had a lot of respect for his neighbour. She was a strong, independent woman.

"So what did they tell me?" she asked, musing. "They kept talking about 'Hen's Chicken' and seemed really pleased with themselves."

Mickey nodded. The letters and lealfets he had brought back with him were spread out on the table.

"Henshykan?" he prompted.

She nodded, and put her own collection of paper out in a line.

"The thing is," she started again, "I was talking to middle management, people who worked for the Council. Some of them in the Planning Department. They were celebrating, as if they'd pulled off a good deal."

Mickey was baffled. The people she was talking about, they were Civil Servants, weren't they? What kind of deal -

"They have shares in the company, Henshykan," she said.

Mickey looked aghast.

People who worked for the Council - Well, they had to 'declare an insterest', didn't they? If they owned shares -

"They were talking about the shopping precinct down on Regent Road, the one you're interested in," she said. "It's a 'billion dollar deal', they said, and laughed. It's a 'decade of development'. It's a huge profit for the company."

"And the shareholders will benefit," Mickey mused. Any shareholders, even Council employees.

"It's worse than that," Denise confided. "There's another link. Their pension scheme, Manchester Boundaries Pension Association, has shares in Henshykan, lots of them. If the developers make a profit, then the Council workers get a bigger pension."

Mickey absorbed that news, culled from drunken boasters in a seedy Club in Manchester. No offence, Denise.

"Do you believe them?" he asked. "All the things they said?"

"Not all," she agreed, admitting a possibility of things that needed to be proved. "Some men lie," she said.

"You know," he said slowly, "we used to worry about people in positions of influence being bribed. We thought they might be handed 'little brown envelopes', stuffed with cash. This is a lot more sophisticated. It's a New World, Den."

She sighed. "It's an incentive for the dogs to let the fox into the henhouse, isn't it?"

Mickey sighed. He didn't like to think of himself as a hen. He would rather be a fox, any day.

Denise said: "I didn't want to do it, but I asked the guys with loose lips about OUR development, out there, on the Playing Fields. They'd heard about it, Mickey, but it's small potatoes. That doesn't mean it won't go through. There's already a lot of steam behind it, and when the plan is finally presented, there will be nobody against it, nobody with any power. Just us."

Mickey showed the glossy leaflets he had collected.

"I've been to Billy's flat to collect his mail," he said. "All these letters, and all this bumf, it's all about the plan to demolish the man's flat and construct a twenty-story tower above it."

The problem for Mickey, which he didn't want to burden Denise with, is that the plan included the whole block, including Melia's building, on the other road. The whole lot, including other shops and stores, faced demolition.

Mickey said: "The strategy is the same. The developers know that the government is happy for them to build on 'brownfield sites', so the company spends a lot of time running down the existing buildings. In Billy's case, they're saying that the 'Victorian sewers' under the site have to be replaced. Oh, yeah? So why not flatten everything that's there, clear the site, fix the sewers and then replace - but with twenty stories not three or four. Only problem? If the bricks and mortar are cleared, so are the existing residents."

"Slightly different here," Denise pointed out. "Those playing fields have a value to local schools and football clubs, so they've had to promise to find space for them elsewhere. Meanwhile, the 'oh, so poor people', with their need for five and six bedroomed houses are going to be happy with the new development. It 'meets a need' in the city. The Council gets to see them housed - "

"And our lives are blighted," Mickey agreed, thinking of all the disruption that building works would bring.

Then, thinking about it, he added: "Same strategy down Regent Road. The developers spend ages trying to convince us that the existing shops have no value, and then include a vague promise that 'retail will be included' in the new development. Of course, that will mean expensive shops and restuarants, no use to existing residents. They will lose affordable shopping."

"Any objection is met with a vague promise," she said. "The only definite thing about all of this, is cramming as many units into the ground available and selling at the highest price. There's always a vague promise of 'affordable homes' being included, but how often does that arrive? Something happens along the way, and 'affordable' gets lost."

Mickey thought about it.

Looking from outside, objectively, it was obvious that big developers like Henshykan were getting their own way, all the time. All they had to do was talk positive, stress so-called 'benefits' and sit back and watch as their plans went through.

It was as though the people of Salford, the residents and the politicians, were being invited to put their heads in a noose, and they were doing it willingly. They were agreeing to being fooled. They were being cheated by consent.

The much valued 'Section 106' money was another example. He had seen down on the Crescent how a development had included a promise of a massive donation to the local community, and then it had never materialised. Something about 'contingencies' and losing 'normal profits'. The Council, strangely, had allowed that to happen, willingly.

So, he was amazed that the men he had met earlier in the day were promising to put a million 'up front'. That had never happened before, he was sure! But what would happen then - after the million had be used to tempt the 'kidnappers', - then, if the police caught the 'bad guys', the bag of cash would be taken back and put into Henshykan's coffers? Would it ever come out again?

"It's all right for me, Mickey," Denise was saying. "I've got savings. I can buy elsewhere. I can move. What about you?"

I've got savings, Mickey was thinking. I can move.

So can Melia.

But that wasn't really the point, was it?

Chapter TWELVE: The Green Out

It was the hottest day of the year.

It wasn't so bad when Mickey was driving down to the church that morning - the air con in the car was quite sufficient - but when he parked and stepped out, the hot air hit him. It was like stepping into a furnace, most unusual for England.

It wasn't even noon. It promised to get hotter later. But Mickey was keen to be early. When there's a million dollars sitting in the building in a carpet bag, there were so many things that might go wrong.

Especially with Inspector de Angelis in charge.

Mickey hadn't seen the eccentric policeman for days. They hadn't talked. Mickey was uncertain about the plan.

At the door, the Church Warden was propping up the wall. Waiting for someone?

"Can I make you a tea or a coffee, young man?" he said amiably, then led the way into the building.

Mickey followed the man inside, then turned left to the kitchen. The man went round the back and Mickey stood at the counter. Somebody was already in, boiling a kettle. She turned, and welcomed Mickey with a smile.

A Vicar. Some kind if Church of England person, with a white collar and black clothes.

"Is this your church?" Mickey asked cheerfully.

She demurred.

"I've got a church in Trafford," she said, "across the river. But I brought the fans."

Mickey turned and noticed that there were two or three fans on stands against the far wall, and helpers seemed to be setting up another one. They were about five feet high, and the kind that swished gently from side to side. It was cooling the interior.

Mickey accepted a cup of coffee and went to sit down at a small table opposite.

"Not there," a stern voice told him. "That's for Food Club."

Mickey saw that a woman was sitting to his right. She had a cash box open on her own table, and a ledger.

"If you want to join it's five pounds," she told him. "Then, every week, it's three pounds for ten items."

There were a number of people waiting. One by one they were called into a side room on the other side of the main door, and allowed to pick ten items. Not a Food Bank, where items are free. A Club, where you have to pay, but so little, it was a great help.

Impressed, Mickey looked for a seat on the left, along the wall.

There were two men in blue serge uniforms. Police? No, Security Guards.

He sat down next to one of them. The man had been watching Mickey.

"We made the same mistake, mate," he said sympathetically. "It's Saturday morning, and the Food Club is on."

"Takes priority," the other one said.

Mickey nodded. Fair enough. It would finish before the meeting this afternoon.

"You here for the cash?" he asked the pair.

They nodded. One said: "We brought the carpet bag in our armoured vehicle. It's parked out back."

Mickey asked: "Why you waiting?" Surely, their job was done.

The other man chuckled. "We think we might be called on to take it away again. With all these people, milling about - well, do you think the kidnappers are going to show? There's police inside, as well."

'Inside'? Inside the church.

Mickey and the Security Guards were sitting at the back of the building, in the screened off 'community hall'. The actual 'church' part, on the left, looked dark and mysterious. Cool perhaps, cooler than this half.

Mickey had been told that at the last meeting, the speakers' table had been placed across the door between the two halves. But this time, a table was in front of him, on the right hand side of the hall, with a line of chairs in front. That means there was room for a walkway between that line and the chair Mickey was sitting on. People had easy access from the door, straight through to the church. In case they needed to get in, like the Security guards, or out - like as if they needed to make a fast exit.

Mickey asked: "Policemen here? Inside the church?"

The Security men nodded. One said: "You're not meant to notice them. They're in plain clothes."

The humourous one said: "I've never seen such 'plain' clothes! You think a Hawaian shirt and red shorts are 'plain' clothes?"

Why not wear shorts on such a sweltering day, Mickey was thinking.

But if that was Mr Dee de Angelis, then that was something he wanted to see. The Inspector had never worn casual wear in his presence.

He finished his coffee and put the mug under the chair, then walked casually up to the church door.

Mickey could see people through the glass.

Yes, there was a Hawaian shirt at the front of the pews, and two men in less loud shirts to Mickey's right, at the back.

One of them got to his feet, maybe because he spotted Mickey, and came out of the door.

"You're Sergeant Fellowes's mate, right? I thought I recognised you."

Mickey nodded. Yeah, Don was Mickey's best friend, of many years, but they hadn't seen each other for a while.

"I'm just going for another coffee," the policeman said. "Walk with me."

Mickey noticed that the man was in white shirt and dark trousers. 'Plain clothes'? Not really. He'd probably just taken his jacket and tie off. It wasn't going to fool any criminals. Mickey wondered who they were expecting.

The policeman was happy to talk.

He said: "Look, we're just following orders. We're from Central station in Manchester. We were told to get down here and watch the money. But we don't know the Plan, whatever it is. We don't even know the Inspector - wherever he's from."

They were standing in front of the kitchen counter, and the man was handed two cups by the lady Vicar.

"Inspector de Angelis?" Mickey prompted. "He's not from your station."

"Not our Division," the man said. "Neither of us have worked with him before. Maybe if he was wearing his uniform, we could tell by his number where he's from. But that outrageous Pacific shirt tells us nothing."

You could ask him, Mickey was thinking but understood. If these two cops were mere constables, they wouldn't want to question an Inspector. Even if they had questions, it was above their pay grade.

"You must have been told something!" Mickey protested.

"Look, we sit at the back, and if anyone tries to sieze the money, we jump on them and arrest them."

"Where's the money?"

"Under the altar."

It was a small church, Mickey was thinking. Not the building, but the congregation. There was an original altar at the far end, the east end of the nave, with glorious stained glass windows and tapestries either side. But a new altar had been set up, down the steps and on the floor. More intimate, less challenging, if there was only a small group of people each Sunday.

The policeman strolled back to his pal, with cups in his hands. Mickey opened the door for him, helpfully.

He thought about going down and talking to the Inspector, but if he was on Observations duty -

Mickey turned and walked back to the seat next to the Security guards. He sat down.

Things seemed cooler.

He saw that a helper had put two table-top fans either side of the table opposite, presumably the one where the Honoured Guests would be sitting. Also, there was an oscillating fan at the entrance to the Food Club room now.

Mickey hearly jumped out of his skin.

Paolo McCully was standing there, watching.

Mickey hurried over, trying to be unobtrusive.

"Outside!" he muttered.

They exited the main door, and turned left, towards the flowers, trees and lawn. They didn't sit down.

"What are you doing here?" Mickey demanded. "You're meant to be one of the kidnapped few. If they think you've escaped, then there's no need to hand over any millions to supposed kidnappers."

"We know it's fake," the Trade Unionist said easily, "and soon everyone is going to know. But that won't stop us taking the cash."

"You have a plan?"

"There's a back door to the church, behind the old altar. It's where the Priest used to come in, from his house. I've got half a dozen Union guys waiting. Big, beefy guys. They play rugby. At my signal, they're going to rush in, overwhelm the few police people, and rush out with the money. We've got a car waiting. We'll be out before anyone notices, even."

"When?"

"Before the meeting starts. Maybe at noon, when the Food Club starts to wind up."

He turned, as if he had finished the conversation.

"Wait!" Mickey growled. "I want to know one thing. What happened to Billy Budman?"

Paolo sighed. "Yeah, that was a tragedy. The problem was, he wanted it. He wanted to come on the minibus. Then, when we got to the Eco Forest Retreat, he wanted to stay, even though he hadn't brought his medication. Then, when we suggested going into town and getting a prescription, he wanted to stay put, not run the risk of being spotted."

"He wanted to die?" Mickey said acidly.

"He wanted to take the risk. He had a couple of seizures, but it didn't look too serious. Then, one morning, we found him in bed."

"He 'wanted' to go into the reservoir?"

"He did. He said that, one night, when we were sitting around the campfire. He said he didn't want to be buried."

There was a law against it, Mickey knew. They hadn't informed the authorities someone had died, that was an offence, and they'd tried to dispose of a body, unlawfully. It wouldn't bring Billy back, but still -

Mickey's phone rang. While he tried to answer it, Mr McCully made his escape.

It was Caulfield.

He wasn't in a good mood.

"Haven't you got my messages?" he asked curtly. "Just because I'm out here in Australia - "

"Yeah, sorry," Mickey mumbled. "Can I help you?"

"No," Richard Caulfield said forcefully. "I can help YOU. Look, when I was on the video call that time, you cut the connection, just as a man came into the room. I caught a glimpse of him. I think you were calling him 'Inspector'. That ring any bells?"

Mickey nodded. "Inspector de Angelis. You saw his face?"

"I did, and I thought I remembered him from somewhere. Well, the answer is - right here! You may call him 'de Angelis', but his real name is Johnny Angel. He's wanted in three Australian states, for fraud and confidence tricks."

"He's a Con Man?"

"Every bone in his body."

Mickey was stunned. He stared at the phone in disbelief. He had been fooled, so completely?

Caulfield said: "It's the middle of the night here, I'm not going to stop and chat. I just wanted to be helpful."

"Yeah, yeah. Thanks, Richard," Mickey said, although he never called him that.

"One last thing," the ex-Deputy Director told Mickey. "Captain knew it. Or, at least, suspected he was dirty. That's why he put you two togehter."

Oh great, Mickey was thinking. I was expected to work it out for myself!

Mickey put his phone away, slowly, thoughtfully, then he turned and hurried back into the church.

It was like walking into a wind storm.

There were fans to the left, fans to the right. Fans on the table. The blasts were sweeping across the room.

It was certainly working. The temperature was way down on the outside, practically chilly, but Mickey was disorientated.

He walked forward, looking for his two new friends from the Security company.

They were standing next to the door into the church, arguing with somebody.

It was the man Mickey knew as 'Inspector de Angelis'.

"I'll take it," he was shouting, and he had a carpet bag in his hand.

"It's our responsibility," the first Security guy was saying. "We've got the van outside. It is secure."

Mickey strode up, barging into the conversation.

"What's happening?" he demanded.

"Don't get involved in this, Something," the 'Inspector' said. "Nobody's showed. It's time to leave."

With the money?

The Security guys were making it clear they thought this wasn't 'protocol', and were trying to refute the idea.

Behind the 'Inspector', the two policemen - in plain clothes - were standing, looking helpless. They still thought this man in a colourful shirt was their superior, and they couldn't argue with him.

Mickey looked around for help, desperately.

Where was Paolo and his rugby team? There was no sign of them.

"Now, if you'll excuse me, I need to get out of here and make this money safe," the so-called 'de Angelis' was saying.

He was brushing everyone off, and heading for the main door.

"Don't run, Johnny," Mickey shouted. "We know who you are!"

The plain clothes 'Inspector' turned and saw that Mickey was serious.

He was rumbled.

It was clear he would have to run.

"Stop that man! He's a thief," Mickey yelled, hoping somebody would assist.

The Church Warden came waddling out from behind the kitchen counter with the biggest knife Mickey had ever seen.

He bore down on the fake policeman, the carving knife held high. Johnny Angel held the carpet bag up the side of his face to defend himself, and the knife plunged through the thin fabric. Johnny tried to pull free and the bag ripped from stem to stern.

Fresh new fifty dollar bills cascaded out into the air, and some fell on the floor.

The powerful air currents of the fans swept them up, blowing in the wind, forming a blizzard of green currency.

People coming out of the Food Club door recognised an opportunity and started grabbing cash out of the air. Some people, newly arrived, fell to their knees and scooped bundles off the floor. There was yelling and greedy screaming.

Well, Mickey was thinking, at least the money is going to the residents of the area.

That was some justice.

THE END

Other Books by Mike Scantlebury

(Author of Scanti-Noir)
The Amelia Hartliss Mystery series
Book One: Poison Doctor
Book Two: Hartliss Running
Book Three: Prince William (At Olympics 2012)
Book Four: Con-Fusion
Book Five: Mayors' Tales
Book Six: Secret Garden Festival 2012
Book Seven: Kidnapping Cameron
Book Eight: Secret Garden 2013
Book Nine: Fresh Heir
Book Ten: The Golden Chip
Book Eleven: The Folksinger 2013
Book Twelve: Salford World War
Book Fourteen: Salford Trenches
Book Fifteen: Terror Beach
Book Sixteen: A Shot at Mayor
Book Seventeen: JC's Cure for Cancer
Book Eighteen: Arms it is
Book Nineteen: People Say Stuff
Book Twenty: Everybody Lies
Book Twenty One: Co-Vid 2020
Book Twenty Two: Co-Vid 2020, Part 2
Book Twenty Three: C0-Vid 2020, Part 3
Book Twenty Four: Co-Vid 2020, Part 4
Book Twent Five: Tales Of Old Buile Hill
The Mickey from Manchester series
Book One: Black and White
Book Two: Off The Rails
Book Three: A Limp Piccolo
Book Four: Filling In
Book Five: New, Clear Future
Book Six: Housing Erases Debts
Book Seven: The Bone Key Curse
Book Eight: Multimedia (*BBC comes to Salford*)

Book Nine: Lucky Ignatius
Book Ten: Reverend Dumb
Book Eleven: Jennercide
Book Twelve: Lethal Election
Book Fourteen: Trumps A Mayor
Book Fifteen: Senctioned
Book Sixteen: 75 Years
Book Seventeen: Globoil Marxits
Book Eighteen: Global Markets, Part 2
Book Nineteen: The Great British Fake Housing Crisis
Book Twenty: Housing Crisis, Part 2
Book Twenty One: Housing Crisis, Part 3
Book Twenty Two: Housing Crisis, Part 4
Book Twenty Three: Korruption Kills
Book Twenty Four: Korruption Kills, Part 2
Book Twenty Five: Korruption Kills, Part 3
Book Twenty Six: Korruption Kills, Part 4

Don't miss out!

Visit the website below and you can sign up to receive emails whenever Mike Scantlebury publishes a new book. There's no charge and no obligation.

https://books2read.com/r/B-A-SODI-OWMWE

BOOKS 2 READ

Connecting independent readers to independent writers.

About the Author

Mickey is from Manchester, and he's a Tough Guy. My name is Mike Scantlebury and I'm the author. I'm not a tough guy, I'm more like an opal, small and perfectly formed. But - more bad news, and worse than that - I'm from Bristol, which is a small, historic port in South West England. It's only claim to fame is that people sailed from there in the 15th century and discovered America. Oh, yeah, well, that is quite a Big Thing, isn't it? But that's the deceptive part of the whole story. I live in Salford now, across the river from the big Northern city of Manchester. My 'Manchester' is not like anyone else's, and if you think you know Manchester - maybe from reading other books set there, or seeing the place on films or on television - I need you to know that. Things aren't always what they seem, are they? Luckily, Manchester has Mickey, which means, fortunately for them, that whenever something bad happens, (and it does, regularly), they've got someone who is going to come in, do The Right Thing, and clear up the mess. Not every town can say that now, can they?

Read more at www.Salford.me.

Milton Keynes UK
Ingram Content Group UK Ltd.
UKHW030049020924
447747UK00001B/2